TAMARA PALMER

MISSING TYLER

MISSING TYLER

Tamara Palmer

Santel ePublishing
Santa Barbara, California
http://www.santelepublishing.com

Publisher's Note: This is a work of fiction. Names, characters, places, and incidents are a product of the author's imagination. Locales and public names are sometimes used for atmospheric purposes. Any resemblance to actual people, living or dead, or to businesses, companies, events, institutions, or locales is completely coincidental

Proofread/Copyedit: www.ProofreadNZ.co.nz
Book design: Judith Sansweet
Cover design: Catherine McDonough
Photographer: Annette Patko

MISSING TYLER/ Tamara Palmer — 1st ed.
ISBN 10 1542884705
ISBN 13 9781542884709

What readers have to say:

"*Missing Tyler* is an absolute gem. This novel is a tender, heartfelt, and deeply honest story of death, grief, recovery, and love. It's one of the few books I've encountered that so honestly takes on the essential issues surrounding an untimely and tragic death: the effects on family, questions about the afterlife, explorations of grief, and ways to recalibrate one's life. Those alone are many gifts; but the novel also offers humor and joy and love -- all the complexities of the human heart. This novel shares a beautiful story, writing, and soul.

Laura Pritchett, author of *Making Friends with Death*

"With the explosion of young adult novels out there, *Missing Tyler*, by talented writer Tamara Palmer, belongs in the category of "you must absolutely read." The story pulls you into the many undiscovered feelings these believable young characters experience. Tremendous loss and the grieving process, young love that many can identify with, and the struggles of adult relationships that slowly become unglued are portrayed and experienced. Seamlessly, Tamara ties everything together to allow the reader to be swept along on the waves of emotions encountered in the roller coaster of life, and then be left with comforting cool breezes to anticipate the next event."

Marla Roth-Fisch Award-winning author/illustrator,
Sensitive Sam series

"Tamara Palmer has done a captivating job of absorbing the reader in a recognizable journey of grief, loss, and teenage angst. This young adult novel takes the reader though a healthy grieving process with grace and resilience, and includes an amazing modeling of strength that offers significant lessons in how to recover from our own losses. Despite the topic of death that underlies the story, the author makes the journey pleasurable and suspenseful. As a psychologist, I highly recommend this book to anyone working on recovering from the loss of a loved one, or who would just enjoy a good read."

Lisa Page, Psy.D.

"Heartbreaking, real, witty and powerful all at the same time. A debut novel of surviving heartbreak in your family while navigating growing up and accepting change. Tamara Palmer does a good job of capturing the teenage personality of all the characters, and we can feel Kit's struggles as she experiences growth through the pain of losing her twin brother, Tyler. The Jewish traditions and rituals in the book, and the extended family with normal struggles help the reader clearly see Kit's full world."

T. King, Teacher Librarian – Cresthill MS

Dedication

This book is dedicated to a boy I never met. In my childhood, I overheard adults sharing a story of a boy who'd been struck and killed while riding his bike. Graphic details of the description of his death haunted me for years. Eventually those memories, like embers, sparked a novel. With this book, I honor his spirit. He is unknown, but never forgotten.

To Janeen:
May Kit take you
on a fantastic
journey!

Chapter One

The limousine arrived at 10:00 a.m. sharp. From where I was sitting on the porch swing, I watched the driver comb his hair as he looked in the rearview mirror and pick at the spaces between his teeth. Then I eyed a half-eaten poppy seed bagel on the dashboard. Poppy seed, our favorite. Correction: *my* favorite. Correction, correction, correction!

Scream, scream, sigh!

Ugh.

He slid out of the limo, all smooth and elegant-like, palming the wrinkles out of his jacket, and straightening his tie. His face was heavy with sadness, an emotion I imagined him applying like makeup, before he left for work.

I didn't need him to be sad. He didn't know us. Tyler was no one to him. This was just his job. Day in and day out, he took people to bury their dead.

The driver paced himself – like he knew he was early, which he was. Slowly, he approached our whitewashed brick steps, faded by the sun and salt air. Carefully, and with great effort, he climbed each one. I detected a bit of a limp, like he had a bad leg. When he got to the top, he cleared his throat, took a deep breath, and knocked on our front door.

"They probably can't hear you," I huffed, rocking back and forth on the swing. Its rusted metal chain scraped against itself begging for more grease, or more likely, to finally be retired.

"Oh! I'm sorry, little lady. I didn't see you there," he jumped a bit and I felt bad. He maintained his practiced politeness, hands held behind his back, his gaze angled downward.

Please dear sir, I wanted to scream, stop with the affected air of grief. It's unbearable to watch. Just be you. You're allowed to be happy. Please won't someone be happy?

"They're on the back porch," I told him, lazily pointing my arm to the side of our house where a broken brick path would lead him under the archway to my parents and Grandma. He tipped his hat at me, said nothing more, and walked down the stairs, disappearing around the side of our house.

I continued to swing, pulling my legs to my chest. The fuzz of my unshaven legs tickled my arms and caused an unpleasant tingly sensation to spread over my body. I pulled my dress around my legs to make it stop, and against the swing's desire for stillness, I pushed myself faster. And then, as if the swing launched me into an alternate universe, I was back on the playground in grade school and I could see and hear Tyler pushing me on the swings, screaming, "Faster, Kit, faster! Flip over the top bar! I know you can do it!" and I closed my eyes, wishing I could flip myself out of this world to be with him again.

✳ ✳ ✳ ✳

The driver returned with the family procession tagging behind him. As they reached the limo, I heard them calling to me. I didn't want to leave my swing for the suffocating tomb of a car. Leaving would mean it was all really happening. Like an activated stopwatch, leaving would start everything.

I dreamed myself an angel — my body floating effortlessly off the swing and down the steps. In reality, though, I stumbled my way to the car. The high heels I fought with Mom to wear killed my feet. I should have listened to her and worn my flats. My black sundress billowed in the light breeze and my orange scarf floated up to tickle my face. Mom called the orange "inappropriate," when I put it on this morning, but she didn't have any fight left in her to tell me to take it off. Had she already forgotten that it was Tyler's favorite color? What else had she forgotten? I'd never forget anything.

I closed my eyes for a second, trying to drown in the sensation of the scarf dancing across my face as I walked across the sidewalk to the street.

"Dammit!" I screamed, as my knee collided with the door of the limousine.

"Kit, watch your mouth." Mom shot me her usual Watch your manners! glare, which ended up looking more like a cry of despair than anything else. It was only as an afterthought that she reached down to pat my knee and make sure I was okay.

Inside the limousine, I tried to sink into the cool, black, leather seat. I didn't hyperventilate like I worried I would. I was too numb. My first limo ride: I always thought it would have been to my prom. But here I was, on the way to bury my brother.

✳ ✳ ✳ ✳

At the cemetery, we all took comfort in the shade of the tent. I grabbed on tight to my grandmother's pale, soft hand – and kept a watchful eye on Dad. His normally tanned face was blank and colorless, making it look like he too had been cut out of his time on Earth, but had forgotten to tell his body. The service dragged on and on. I tried to focus on what the rabbi was saying, but most of it was in Hebrew, and hell if I knew what any of it meant. The chanting tones only lulled me into a deeper fog.

Deep in that trance, I was suddenly back on summer break after fourth grade. I saw Tyler and me racing our bikes, pretending we were in the Tour de France. I was Laurette L'fantastique and he was Laurence L'superb. We would time our laps, usually coming out neck-and-neck, but then, in the end, he'd win that race — always a step faster, a step stronger, a step out of reach.

* * * *

I closed my eyes while they lowered the casket into the grave. I heard the heavy groan of the weight sinking into the ground, and a sudden wave of nausea overcame me. A hint of puke crept up my throat and I was worried that I might really be sick. Mom's heavy sobs drowned out the violinist. In spite of it all, I was acutely aware of Dad's silence behind me.

The past few days lingered in my mind: the reporters, the television crews, the hospital, Tyler's mangled bike. That phone call. That awful phone call.

Standing in front of Tyler's grave, it was Brandon, Tyler's best friend, who was there to console me. His hand gently rubbed my back. I wanted so badly to feel the pain of my sunburn from just last week when Tyler and I spent too much time goofing off in Brandon's pool.

Aunt Deborah gave me a stiff nudge. It was my turn to throw dirt onto the casket. The lump in my throat fell like a rock into my stomach as I reached for the shovel. I couldn't do it. I couldn't have any part in burying him. I hadn't agreed to this.

The casket was barely visible from where I stood looking down into the open grave. A few shovelfuls of dirt were already beginning to cover the beautiful mahogany. All day, my mind had been picturing him lying in there, hot and sweaty. No air. I started coughing uncontrollably while beads of sweat ran down my face. I could feel all of my relatives' eyes on me as I begrudgingly lifted the shovel. The weight of it was more than my shaky arms could bear. A shudder rippled through the crowd. I looked down in horror. The shovel had fallen in.

The world faded to grey, then turned black.

✳ ✳ ✳ ✳

I awoke to find myself in the backseat of the limousine. My head was in Brandon's lap and he was patting wet paper towels on my forehead.

"What happened?" I asked, clutching my aching temples.

"You passed out," Brandon said as he continued to cool my face. The paper towels felt heavenly.

"Where are we?"

"We're still at the cemetery. We'll be heading to your Aunt Deborah's pretty soon. It's almost done."

"I missed the rest of it?" I tried to sit up but everything rippled grey again.

"Hey, hey, chill." Brandon laughed, gently but very firmly pushing me back down.

"My head is killing me."

"Just try to relax," he said, staring blankly out the window.

I tried. Brandon's chocolate eyes melted as his gaze remained fixed on the gravesite, probably looking for that lost piece of himself.

Brandon and Tyler, the magic duo since Mrs. Klein's kindergarten class at Bridgeview Elementary. The two of them doing monkey bar races at the school playground. On weekends, burying me in the sand at Jefferson Avenue beach. And almost every day of grade school screaming, "Get out!" as I snuck into the basement when they played at our house.

"NO GIRLS ALLOWED!"

"But I can be the girl pirate," I pleaded, peeking through the wood railing.

"No girl pirates allowed!"

"But what if I were ..."

"Go away, Kit!"

Brandon and Tyler. Tyler and Brandon.

"I'm actually glad Crissy couldn't make it," I admitted to Brandon, attempting to cover my dislike of his girlfriend with my need to grieve. "I needed to be your priority today."

Brandon looked down and smiled, his hand making lazy figure eights on my forehead.

I closed my eyes and saw Tyler. The same movie was on, as it had been for a few days now, playing on an endless loop against the backs of my eyelids.

We were five or six years old and sharing a bedroom. I had the bottom bunk. I woke up screaming in the middle of the night from a nightmare. Tyler started screaming too and slid down the ladder, like a fireman who'd gotten the midnight call. He climbed into my bed and held me tight.

"Sshh ...," he whispered to me like Mom often did. "Don't cry Kit, don't cry. I'm here. It's just a dream."

✻ ✻ ✻ ✻

After the gravesite, we all met at Aunt Deborah's house for the start of shiva, the Jewish week of mourning. I guess shiva is technically supposed to be at your own house, but Aunt Deborah insisted that she host it, and Mom does whatever Aunt Deborah says.

The house was abuzz with pesky, fly-like people, crying and hugging one another. I was drowning in the overwhelming grief of it all. From the second I made my entrance, I was passed like a toy doll from relative to relative, many of whom I couldn't remember ever meeting. Funerals and weddings, that's what brings family together, they say.

The house dated back to the Victorian era, a fact Aunt Deborah didn't let anyone miss. Tyler and I liked to refer to it as being on the hysterical — as opposed to historical — society registry. It was like being in the world's most boring, musty museum. Knickknacks and pictures covered almost every square inch of furniture, and it was impossible to set down a glass without having to move something. The antiques seemed so fragile, I couldn't help fearing that one false move would send something priceless crashing to the floor — and I'd had my share of near-misses.

There was the time Tyler threw a ball to Aunt Deborah's son, Ari, in the living room, and Ari, being totally incapable of anything that involved coordination, missed and it went crashing into a figurine. Tyler had to pay out of his allowance to replace it, even though it was totally Ari's fault.

"Kit, you remember your cousin, Mordechi? He lives outside Baltimore?" It was more of a statement than a question as Aunt Deborah tugged on my arm and drew me in close to her, placing me on display like an interactive part of the museum: "Kit Carlin here, now to tell you about the boring tchotchkes in the dining room."

"Hi," I mumbled. Mordechi had grey tufts protruding from his ears and a horrible comb-over — a vain attempt to hide his bald spot. I wasn't sure how someone with grey hair could technically be a cousin and not a great-uncle. Maybe he was a great-cousin. Does that even exist?

"What a little angel you've grown up to be. Let me get a good look at you ... Ah, yes, you look so much like your mother did at that age, such beautiful dark hair and deep green eyes. You're going to be quite the heartbreaker."

I rolled my eyes at Aunt Deborah, and she gave me that smile of hers, the one that said, Just play along, dear.

"So tell me again, how old you are?"

"Fifteen," I answered, while my eyes scanned the room over Mordechi's head. Where had Brandon gone? I needed him to rescue me. Damsel in distress! Damsel in distress! Aunt Deborah placed an arm around my waist, squeezing my side in that thanks for being sweet way, but squeezed a tad too tightly and I gasped a little at the shock of pain. Apparently no one noticed. Of course.

"Such a tragic day. Such loss, such loss ..." he said in a creepy tone that made me think that something else had happened and I was about to find out what it was.

My head nodded in mute agreement as my eyes darted around the room searching for an escape route. Where was Grandma Carlin? Where were Mom and Dad? Were they off somewhere putting on a normal show? I couldn't anymore. My acting abilities had maxed out.

"Well, you take care." He extended his arms for a hug. I leaned over, offering only half a hug, my shoulders against his. His onion breath could have made a flower wilt. Aunt Deborah smiled from across the room as I walked away. A few minutes later, I heard her call, "Tiffany, you remember Mordechi?" as she walked the next visitor his way.

I walked purposefully, seeking out Brandon and doing my best to avoid eye contact with the other guests. At the far side of the kitchen, I spotted him, cornered by some little old lady who I think used to work with Mom.

"Now, you're Katrina's boyfriend, right?" I heard her ask and I tried not to laugh. Brandon's type was curvy, blond, bubbly, and cheerleadery — aka Crissy — and I was built like a plank: rail thin, barely any boobs, long black hair, and no bubble or cheer in me. I couldn't have been further from any notion of a girlfriend.

I heard Brandon answer, "No. I'm ... I mean, I was Tyler's best friend," as he pushed a lock of blonde hair out of his eyes, then coughed. He always coughed when he was nervous.

Brandon was letting his hair grow out so it was in that in-between, awkward stage where it wasn't long enough to look cool or short enough to look stylish. No matter what length his hair was, though, there was no doubt that he and

Tyler were the true heartbreakers of our high school. I swear that girls would follow them around like they were famous.

I loved teasing him, "Can I have your autograph, Brandon?" while I'd batted my eyelashes at him. If I ever did that at his house though, I usually ended up in the pool — whether in a bathing suit or fully clothed, it never mattered.

"Oh good, kids are dating way too young these days." The old lady mumbled something else under her breath and looked in my direction. "Why, there's Katrina now!"

"Yeah, it's me." God, I needed to get out of this house! "Brandon, I've been looking for you."

I could tell he was relieved to see me. He flashed his widest smile, which always triggered a dimple.

"So are you enjoying being tormented by my amazingly bizarre family?" I asked as I led him away.

"Oh, they're fine. She was sort of sweet. Asked me the same question three times in five minutes, but that's what old ladies do. My Aunt Grace is the same way. Who is she, anyway?"

"I think she used to work with my mom. It seems like everyone in our entire life has shown up here. Listen, I'm gonna pass out again if I have to stay in here much longer."

Brandon nodded in agreement. We sighed in unison when we saw the deck swarming with people.

"I know a better way out," I said, leading him through the crowd. "Follow me."

Heading for the basement family room, as we reached the last few stairs, we stopped abruptly. The fireplace mantel was surrounded with pictures of Tyler through the years. There were so many candles it looked like an altar, which was particularly funny in Aunt Deborah's very Jewish home.

I lost my footing stepping off the stairs and plopped right down on the new carpet that lacked the cushion of the seventies shag they had finally gotten rid of.

9

Brandon came from behind me and lifted me to my feet. He propped me against the wall so I was looking right at him; then, when he noticed fresh tears, he took a wad of something out of his pants pocket and moved it toward my face.

"Gross! Is that toilet paper?" I forced a laugh through my tears as I pushed his hand away.

"Yeah, so what?" he shrugged. "I couldn't find any Kleenex." He shoved the wad into my hand so I could dab at my teary cheeks.

"There's a box right there!" I laughed pointing to the downstairs coffee table. "They're everywhere here."

"Come on, let's look at the pictures." Brandon said, not amused by me calling out his lack of observation.

We walked toward the fireplace, and I kicked off my heels.

"Check this one out. It's you, me, and Tyler at Waves of Wonder in Philly. Remember when he and I tricked you into going down the Spiral of Doom?" Brandon smirked.

"Don't try and cheer me up."

"We want to hear! We want to hear!" A group of kids appeared from the other side of the basement. I forgot that Aunt Deborah still had a play area in the back, even though Ari was seventeen and unlikely to create Lego villages anytime soon.

"Hi, Kit!" Kaleigh exclaimed as she came running at me, then grabbed me in a bear hug.

"Hi," I smiled back. I adored Kaleigh and had been her main babysitter since I first started babysitting. If anyone could cheer me up, it was her.

Brandon looked at me with a grin and a flash in his eye as he started the story. The kids huddled around his feet like it was Saturday afternoon story time at the library. "There's this ride at Waves of Wonder called the Spiral of Doom. Tyler and I had been down it a few times but Kit had never been.

10

We told her that it wasn't as scary as it looked and dared her to go on it, calling her a chicken if she wouldn't."

At that, the kids started snickering and launched into full-on chicken imitations, like they were imagining me with feathers and a cluck in my voice.

"I did go, though," I added, cutting off the cluck-cluck brigade.

"She did," Brandon agreed. The kids' eyes darted between us like they were watching a ping-pong tournament.

"She was wearing this silly bikini and the top came off halfway through the ride! By the time she made it to the end of the slide, she was stuck in the bottom pool with no top! A lifeguard pulled out his bullhorn, turned to Kit, and screamed, 'No one in their right mind wears a bikini to a water park!' They stopped the ride while Kit hid under the water, until someone found a towel for her to wrap herself in. Did they ever find your suit?"

I shook my head. "Nope, it had totally vanished."

The kids hiccupped laughed and I turned beet red, just as I had that day at the park.

"Yeah, that was hilarious," I scowled at Brandon. "How about this one?" I said. "You and Tyler dressed up like monkeys at Halloween. Whose idea was that, anyway?"

"That was all Tyler. For some reason, he was into monkeys that year. I can't remember, though: was that before or after the weasel phase?"

"How about the rat phase? He had rat stationary, toy rats, and then he brought a real one home! Remember that? It completely freaked out Mom! He said he got it at the pet store, but I swear he pulled it out of a gutter."

I was laughing until the guilt choked out the joy and I felt as if I'd tear apart. "How can we be talking about him in the past tense?" I whispered through new tears.

Brandon continued staring at the picture, but I could tell he was tearing up too.

The kids began fidgeting, and I didn't have it in me to say anything to make them feel better. Someone from upstairs called "Emma!" and one of the girls raced up the stairs. Next, "Caleb!" and then one by one, all the kids headed up, and Brandon and I were alone. I settled into the old couch that I'd slept on for so many years on sleepovers. I was shaking my head, but I didn't even know what I was saying no to.

"I brought a flask," Brandon whispered in my ear. I lifted my head out of my hands to see him wiping away his tears with a fresh wad of toilet paper.

"You what?"

"I ditched it under the front porch. It's got Jack Daniels in it. I swiped it from my folks' liquor cabinet. You want some?" Brandon flashed his mischievous grin, the one that made all the girls fall for him.

Right then, Aunt Deborah came down the stairs, calling my name into the expanse of the basement. My eyes dashed around for a place to hide, but as soon as I stood up, she made eye contact with me. She was with another distant relative who looked vaguely familiar. Was it necessary to become reacquainted with my entire family on the worst day of my life? Our family was so enormously huge that I couldn't keep them all straight: second cousins and third cousins and the twice-removed stuff. Forget a family tree — we needed a freakin' forest!

"There you are, Kit. We've been looking for you," she said, coming all the way downstairs. Mom was trailing behind her, with the same glassy-eyed stare she'd had since the phone call. "You remember your dad's cousin, Lorraine." It was more of a statement than a question.

The smell of Mom's perfume triggered a new ripple of sadness. The comfort I'd always taken in that scent was just a stupid illusion. She couldn't really protect me from anything. Maybe once upon a time she could, but not anymore. Hell, she couldn't even protect herself. We were all

12

alone now: me, Dad, Mom, all in our own versions of grief hell, locked in pain.

"I'm sorry to hear about your brother, Katrina," this Cousin Lorraine said as she reached out for a hug. "I can't begin to feel your grief."

I nodded my head like a mute. Why did adults always use your formal name at times like these? I hated my name.

"It's hard to lose a sibling," she continued, "and Tyler was a very special person." She combed my hair away from my face with her fingers, but I jerked back and shook it out so it fell back in my eyes, shielding me like a curtain.

"At least you have your whole summer vacation ahead of you. Heck, before you know it, you'll be back at school and life will be back to normal."

"Normal?!" I screamed — finally at my boiling point. I stomped in a toddler-like temper tantrum to the screen door. "Nothing will ever be normal again!" I screamed again at her, but looked straight at Aunt Deborah. Mom looked the other way, like I was someone else's kid. Someone else's problem.

Brandon came after me, but I pushed him back as I bolted for the farthest reaches of the yard, not caring that I was barefoot and that the ground was covered in pine needles. I ran past a crowd of people sitting at the picnic table, then passed another group of people circling Aunt Deborah's little pond. I didn't stop running until I reached the hammock at the edge of the yard, practically in the woods. If I'd had shoes on, I wouldn't have stopped running.

Snug in the hammock, I closed my eyes and practiced some of the deep breathing Grandma Carlin taught me a few days before when I'd started hyperventilating. I thought back to the campouts we had on so many summer nights. Cousin Ari always got the hammock first. In the middle of the night, though, Tyler would shake me awake. Together we'd wake up Ari, flip him out, and commandeer the hammock for ourselves. Crazy that Ari had already left for Israel for the summer. He'd missed his cousin's funeral.

None of these people really knew Tyler. They said they understood how I felt, but they didn't have a clue! I was his twin sister. Nobody could be closer than that. We shared a bond that they'd never understand. They'd all get to go back to their lives after this. I had to live in this hell forever.

I was sure that somewhere up above, Tyler was looking down and feeling exactly the same way. I looked up at the sky. It was still a deep, crisp blue — not a cloud to be seen. Somewhere, maybe in the treetops, I knew he was smiling. So, with a forced smile and tear-stained eyes, I sniffled and waved back.

"Kit, wake up," Brandon demanded, rocking the hammock and coming dangerously close to tossing me on the pine needles. Slowly, my eyes opened, and then my heart promptly sank. There stood Melissa. She ranked pretty high up the list of People I Didn't Want to See.

Pale was not a tone that suited her well. Her watery eyes, bloodshot with dark circles underneath, made her appear more upset than me and that just amped up my anger.

"Hi, Melissa," I mumbled, wishing I could have drummed up some of the plasticity that the limo driver had, but I'm a bad faker.

"Hi, Kit. I tried to say hi at the funer ..." Her throat caught the last word like a bug. With her monogrammed handkerchief, she delicately wiped away the mascara running down her beautifully painted, rosy cheeks. The pink M on the handkerchief was now black. She carefully held onto a clear plastic cup of sparkling grape juice as though it were expensive crystal instead of a disposable cup from Safeway.

Melissa "Shallow" Katz, Tyler's trophy girlfriend, the queen bee of the rich crowd at Atlantic City High School. Besides showing her off to his friends, I don't know what they could have done together or talked about. Up until this year,

14

Melissa's world never overlapped with ours. She was a Longport girl, and Longport meant money. Mom always said I was just jealous that Tyler was more interested in having a girlfriend than being stuck at home with his sister, but honestly, he could have dated Lindsey Cohen, Kelsey Mayne, Lisa Cavatelli, or any of the other girls who adored him and I would have easily approved. In fact, I would have been excited for him.

Brandon's head hung low, the weight of all this sadness just dragging him toward the ground.

"Crissy really wanted to be here," Melissa started.

"Yeah, I told Kit that Crissy was in Florida at her grandma's," Brandon continued for her. "Her grandma's finally out of the hospital, so Crissy will be back next week."

Crissy was Brandon's on-again, off-again girlfriend and Melissa's BFF. If only Crissy could stay in Florida, maybe even move there, then I could have Brandon all to myself for as long as I needed him. Where Melissa was shallow, Crissy was manipulative. She could work a guy around her little finger, and that's exactly what she'd done to Brandon. Guys ate her up: her confidence, and well, her chest size and reputation. Rumor had it that she'd slept with half the basketball team, even though that had clearly not happened since she'd been with Brandon 80 percent of the year (minus the 20 percent they'd spent broken up for a few days every few months). I felt kind of bad for her on that count. Just where do rumors come from, anyway? Even though Brandon, pretty much like Tyler, could have his pick of any girl in our class, and maybe even the year ahead, it was always Crissy he went back to. They'd been playing out this drama since seventh grade. I was sure he could do better, but what did I really know? I hadn't kissed anyone in over six months, and even then it was Evan Jacobs. On a dare. Did that even count? I certainly hadn't found a guy worth going all the way for.

"Why Tyler?" Melissa asked dramatically, jutting her other hand up into the air as if she were in cheerleading practice. I imagined her yelling "Gimme a T!"

She asked the question as if we all hadn't asked ourselves that same question over and over. I watched as she nervously twirled Tyler's class ring. The yarn that was wrapped around to make it fit her finger had faded with time to a robin's-egg blue.

"You don't mind if I keep it, do you?" she asked, lowering her head and looking up at me like a sad puppy. Minded? Of course I minded! I wanted everything that was Tyler's. Brandon's eyes were practically boring a hole into me so I backed off. For now.

"Yeah, that's fine," I gave in, plotting all the while how I would get it back.

"Thanks, Kit. Brandon said you wouldn't have a problem."

I shot Brandon a look, but he just smiled and rolled his eyes as Melissa leaned over and kissed him on the cheek.

"You're a real sweetheart," she cooed, batting her thick, dark eyelashes. How could she have any mascara left after all the crying? Then I realized: fake lashes.

Melissa fidgeted and I wished she would just disappear. She'd made her appearance. Couldn't she go? Minutes turned into longer minutes and she and Brandon started whispering.

"I'm going to go help your Mom," she said out of nowhere and sashayed away, her shiny blond hair swinging behind her.

"Thank you," I whispered.

"For what?" Brandon smiled.

"For getting rid of her." I fake punched him in the arm. "But I want that ring back."

"I know."

"You better get it back from her."

16

"I will."

"Soon?"

"Geez, Kit!"

"You better, because ..." I began to warn, but before I could finish, Brandon jumped into the hammock, nearly flipping us both out in the process. "Watch your suit!" I cried.

"Who cares?"

"You promise you'll get that ring back? I don't want her to have it."

"Kit, give it up. Listen, we need to get back in the house. Your mom actually sent me out here to find you. I told Melissa to go buy us time."

"I smell booze on your breath."

"Yeah, well, I got tired of waiting for you, so Melissa and I helped ourselves. Want some? You seem like you need some."

"Do you have it with you?"

He pulled the silver flask out from a pocket inside his blazer. I unscrewed the cap and took a swig. The alcohol burned my throat.

"How can you drink that stuff?" I gasped between breaths as I started coughing.

"It tastes better the more you drink," he declared, taking a swing then offering the flask to me again.

"No thanks. I'll handle my pain on my own."

"We should probably head in."

"No. I can't take any more of this sitting shiva shit." I snickered at the sing-song tone. "I've wanted to say that all day." I smiled and Brandon smiled back at me. "But really, I'm sick of all these people. I can't believe this is only the first day. I have to do this all week. Do you think Tyler would want us to sit in this house with the windows closed for days on end? It's summer!"

"Seems weird to me too. What exactly is sitting shiva, anyway? I've been wanting to ask all day, but didn't want to sound dumb." Brandon took another swig from the flask, stretched out in the hammock, and stared up into the sky.

"If you're Jewish, when someone dies, the rest of the family sits shiva. In our case, we're supposed to come back to Aunt Deborah's every day this week and mourn" — I made air quotes when I said mourn — "while friends and other family members come by and pay their respects, you know, and bring food and stuff."

"But I thought just your mom was Jewish."

"Yeah, but in Judaism it doesn't matter if your parents are two different things, you're always what your mother is. And because Dad doesn't care and Aunt Deborah seems to have Mom attached to puppet strings ... we'll be here all week."

Brandon cringed and took another swig. "Gotcha. So if my mom is Methodist and my dad is Presbyterian, does that make me Methodist?"

"I don't know how it works in other religions," I said. "In my opinion, the whole shiva thing is complete bull."

"Have you had to do this before?" Brandon asked, taking yet another swig from the flask and looking so comfortable about it, yet making me more uncomfortable in the process. Was this something he and Tyler used to do together? And, if so, why did I not know?

"Yeah, once, when I was nine years old, I remember going to some relatives' house in Philadelphia when someone died. All of us cousins played in the backyard while the adults sat around the house crying. I was probably like one of those kids in the basement."

Brandon nodded and kept swigging. At this rate, he wasn't going to be able to get out of the hammock.

"Wanna hear something really creepy? Someone told me that if you actually do shiva right, you're supposed to sit with the body for a week," I said.

18

"Woah. That's disgusting. Does anyone do that anymore?"

"Probably. I bet Orthodox Jews do." I eyeballed the flask, wondering if I should give it another try. Brandon didn't see me look and I didn't say anything.

Brandon glanced at his watch and put the booze back in his jacket pocket. "Kit, go back in the house and make your mom happy. I'll be here with you as long as I can. And our friend Jack is here to help anytime," Brandon smiled as he patted his jacket, closed his eyes, and rocked me out of the hammock into a carpet of pine needles.

We didn't make it home that night until after 11 o'clock. Aunt Deborah and Uncle David live on the mainland, in Mays Landing, about a half-hour drive from our house in Margate.

We thanked our neighbors, the Roswells, for watching our house. I still can't believe people actually get robbed while they're at funerals. Mr. Roswell said that several people called and hung up without saying who they were.

There were a bunch of messages, though, and Grandma read them out loud. Cousin Janie from Seattle called to share her condolences, as did one of Dad's old sailing buddies, Bruce, who had just read the obituary. And Dr. Bremer's office called to remind Tyler of his dentist appointment on Monday at 10:30. Mom began to bawl all over again. That got Grandma Carlin and me going, and we reached out for a group hug. Dad looked at us, turned his back, and left the room.

Since that night at the hospital, Dad had done a total 180. He would talk to me, but then walk away before I could respond. He'd taken on an annoying habit of leaving the room when Mom and I started talking. He was in the garage almost all the time now. He was also drinking more, which was weird because Dad was never a big drinker.

It was only in the past few years that Tyler had been old enough to race sailboats with Dad, especially since he was finally nearly as tall. They had plans to sail to Ocean City, in Maryland, in July. Dad was always bragging about Tyler, and Tyler would do anything to make Dad proud. He always told Dad he was going to grow up and race professionally, even take over the family business.

"I'm gonna win the America's Cup for Dad," he used to tell me.

And what was I going to do with my life? Well, it never seemed to matter as much. "Whatever you want to do, honey, I know you'll be great," was about all the interest I could get out of Dad.

The kitchen table was somewhere under all the vases of flower arrangements. The lilies were gorgeous trumpets of orange and yellow. They made me start sneezing, but no one seemed to be left to bless me.

I thumbed through the cards, only half paying attention to who the flowers were from: out-of-state relatives, friends of my folks. There was a huge bouquet of roses. I read the card. It was from Dylan Ryerson, from track at school, and addressed specifically to me: Kit – Thinking of You. Dylan. Dylan was on the team with Tyler and Brandon and me, but I didn't remember him and Tyler being particularly close. The thought of track and our whole group of friends, ugh. At least I could avoid them until next school year.

I collapsed on the couch, turned on the TV, and scrolled through the channels until well after midnight. By the time I made it to bed, I was so exhausted I didn't even bother washing my face or brushing my teeth. But, as tired as I was, my mind wouldn't turn off. As I lay there in the dark, it raced through the birthdays we shared together and the late nights on the boardwalk. I saw us hiding plates of liver and lima beans under our napkins. I imagined us learning to walk. The perfect twins were no longer perfect. With one gone, what was going to happen to the other? Could I even call myself a twin anymore?

I laid in my section of our bunk bed while the other bunk was just beyond the wall in his room — a room I was now forbidden to enter. I curled my body up as tightly as I could and began to shake. Tears were streaming down, falling into salty pools in my mouth, and wetting my pillow. I shook all the images from my head and tried to fall asleep.

Chapter Two

It was Friday, June 9th. I had to constantly remind myself of the day, the month, even the year so I wouldn't get sucked into the timeless hole that was taking over my brain. Technically, there were two more days of finals before my freshman year of high school was over, but under the circumstances, my school had granted me permission to retake finals in August before school started again. In a very unexciting way, my summer vacation had officially arrived.

Back at Aunt Deborah's, the dinner spread had been cleared, making way for the tarts, macaroons, and chocolate desserts that had been brought out every night of shiva.

I'd never forget the first time Brandon ate lox. He had stayed the night with Tyler, and the whole family went out to breakfast the next morning. We ordered two lox platters with extra bagels, and when he realized that the waitress had brought pink, cold, raw fish, he nearly threw up. Somehow, we convinced him to try it. I think Tyler threatened an atomic wedgie or something stupid like that. He ended up loving it, even if he had to close his eyes while he ate it.

Grandma Carlin came into the kitchen dressed in her flowing gypsy pants and poet's blouse, and I caught Aunt Deborah rolling her eyes. Grandma was way too much of a free spirit for Aunt Deborah, who thought Grandma should be dressed in an old lady's black funeral mourning dress. Grandma offered to help clean up, but Aunt Deborah said she had it all under control. Control was Aunt Deborah's middle name.

We usually only saw Grandma on our annual Christmas-break trip to Florida, but she was far and away Tyler's and my favorite relative. Grandma Carlin was ultra-hip. Her apartment bellowed forties' swing music, and it looked out over the ocean. She refused to live in a retirement community, and instead had a super cool condo in South Beach. She always said she wasn't going to rot away in a pre-fab community on a lake in Nowheresville, Florida.

Late Sunday afternoon, we'd hit a lull in visitors and Grandma suggested we sneak off for a walk.

"How about we go get some fresh air?" she asked. "When I was out yesterday, I discovered a lovely trail, by a park not far from here."

I knew exactly the trail she was referring to: it was in the woods where Ari, Tyler, and I used to play pirates. It was the trail I would have taken, had I had shoes on that first day of shiva.

"That sounds great," I said, excited to leave the house. I looked at Aunt Deborah for permission, but she was talking to the inside of the fridge and hadn't heard a word of our conversation. Grandma whispered, "Let's go," and added a conspiratorial wink as we left the house.

"So how are you holding up, kiddo?" Grandma asked.

"All right, I guess."

She took my hand in hers, kissed it, and squeezed it tight. It sounds dorky, but Grandma Carlin was made of pure love. You couldn't help but feel better just being next to her.

"Keep talking to him. He can hear what you're saying. He's not as far away as you might think."

"How do you know I talk to him?" I asked, eyeing her warily. Dad always complained that Grandma had "gone off the deep end, and gotten into all that hippie crap." She simply smiled, and I worried that maybe she had ESP and really could read my thoughts.

"You believe in reincarnation and all that stuff don't you?" I asked.

"Yes, I do."

"So then, what happens to someone when they die? Do they just become a bug or a cow or something?"

"No, no, honey," she giggled, her long, silvery hair glistening in the filtered light. I looked at her and wondered if my hair would be beautiful and silver like hers when I grew old. Then I went and ruined the moment by thinking about how Tyler would never get to grow old. A horrible guilt wound its way through me as I imagined all of the things Tyler wouldn't have a chance to experience, like going to the prom or graduating from high school, let alone getting married and having kids. At least I didn't have to worry about having Melissa as a sister-in-law. That brought a smile.

"The reincarnation that I believe in simply means that a person never dies," she said. "We may leave this human form, but our soul cannot die. We are everywhere, and we stay closest to the ones we love. If I were guessing right, I'd say Tyler is walking beside you nodding in agreement."

I looked beside me, but then felt dumb. Of course he wasn't there.

"I always thought it meant you come back to Earth as an animal," I said, kicking a walnut along the path in front of me. The sun on the back of my legs felt warm and comforting, like a fuzzy blanket.

"Some cultures believe that, and then there are others who think you begin life again as a human. Personally, I have a hard time believing that we jump between animal and human form."

"How do you know about all of this anyway?"

"Oh, back about forty years ago, I began reading books along these lines. It was around the time your grandfather

24

died. I guess I was looking for answers much like you are now. His death more or less shook up my whole belief system."

"So, if I believe in your reincarnation, then Tyler isn't really gone, right?"

"True," Grandma nodded and flashed her big Grandma smile. "It's comforting, isn't it?"

"Yeah," I smiled back. "Yeah, it really is. Well, I know I don't like Judaism, and I hope Mom's not going to make me start going to Temple again." We had to go a lot on Saturday mornings with Ari when we were kids. Tyler and I dreaded every minute of it, especially the parts in Hebrew. Mom only lit the Sabbath candles and said the prayer when Jewish relatives were over for dinner. Dad would play along for Mom, but it's not like he ever converted or anything. We never could figure out why we needed to learn all about Judaism if Mom and Dad were only pretending to believe.

"We all need to find our own truth in our own time."

Grandma and I walked in silence for a while.

"Do you remember when I broke my arm in junior high?" She nodded. We both swatted the air as we walked through a mess of bugs. We were getting close to the pond where Ari, Tyler, and I used to catch frogs. "I was in gym class when it happened, and Tyler came running into the gym holding his arm. He not only knew I was hurt, but he actually felt it in his arm, too."

"I think I remember that, now that you mention it." Grandma reached down to pick up a stone and skipped it perfectly across the pond.

"So, we felt things that happened to the other." I reached for a stone and tossed it, but it sank before the first skip.

Grandma was quiet for a long moment. "Did you feel Tyler's death?" she asked, looking deep into my eyes.

I thought back to that night. Dad and Mom and I were hanging in the living room watching Wipeout on TV. Tyler was at the library studying with friends. Or so Mom and Dad thought. He and Melissa were probably making out under the boardwalk, a block away from the library. The phone rang. Dad answered it. Mom and I kept watching and laughing along as people got knocked off the obstacle course and into a pool of water. Dad yelled "No!" into the phone. Mom jumped to his side and I followed. Dad started crying and Mom asked over and over "What happened? What happened?" When Dad hung up, he couldn't speak. Mom started crying, and I began to pick at my split ends.

He finally said, "We need to go to the hospital," but he was talking to the TV, not to Mom. "Tyler was hit riding his bike."

I finally answered Grandma's question with some of my own. "I remember the numbness, but I didn't feel any pain. Why wasn't there pain? Why didn't I know something had happened? If I didn't feel anything that day, then what does that mean? Shouldn't I have?"

"I don't know, Kit. Maybe he passed so quickly that he didn't have a chance to send any signals to you."

"Maybe." I choked on fresh tears and my legs gave out. Grandma took me in her arms and rocked me where we stood.

When I could finally catch my breath and stand on my own, I said, "I'm scared to never feel that connection again. Now with him gone ..." but that was as far as I could go.

Grandma put an arm around my shoulder and I sank against her, letting my weight dissolve into her hold.

"I'm not going to pretend to completely understand what you're going through, Kit, but I can empathize. While I lost a grandson, which hurts tremendously, you lost your twin brother, the soul you spent nine months with in the womb."

I cried harder and harder and reached into my pockets for the mass of Kleenex that I had stuffed in there before the walk.

Later, we skipped stones on the pond and sat for a while in silence. The heat grew intense, but the sweating had a cleansing effect and I let myself enjoy it as we listened to the birds chirp around us. Life goes on. Birds are hatching and dying. Caterpillars are turning into butterflies and the cycle of life keeps going around and around. The moment felt more peaceful than any of the rabbi's services during shiva. Nature, that's what's real! I looked up, wondering if Tyler was feeling it too, and wishing more than anything in the world that I could have this philosophical conversation with him, right here, right now.

Grandma looked at her watch and then at me. "I wish we could stay here all day," I said.

"We can come back tomorrow. It's getting close to suppertime, though, so we should be getting back."

Before we got too close to Aunt Deborah's house, Grandma pulled me aside and spoke in a low voice. "Let me do some digging. I think I may have some books on spirituality that you'll find interesting. I'll send you a care package when I get back to Florida. It will be our little secret book club," she said, and wrapped me in a Grandma bear hug.

Back at Aunt Deborah's house, people were standing around eating and waiting for the rabbi to arrive. At sunset each day, Aunt Deborah and Uncle David's rabbi gave a half-hour service. It was by far the worst part of the day. The service was entirely in Hebrew and I couldn't understand a thing he said. After suffering through Uncle David's judgmental stares the past few nights, I'd gotten my mouthing down so it actually looked like I was chanting. Mostly, I would pray for Tyler in my head. I talked to him and sometimes I thought I could hear him answer me.

* * * *

Life at our house was quickly becoming a mess. We would get home around nine o'clock each night and had to leave for Aunt Deborah's early the next morning. The mail was piling up, and I knew someone needed to pay the bills.

Grandma Carlin was planning to stay with us for at least three weeks, which would be the most amount of time I'd ever spent with her. Tyler would never get that time with her. Ever.

Grandpa Carlin died when Dad was really little. He was in the Vietnam War. Grandma Carlin's second husband, Pete, died of a heart attack when I was a baby. After that, she said she was done with marriage, that she didn't need the stress of it.

My bubbie and zadie, my Mom's folks, had moved to Israel about five years ago, and now only came to visit every other year. I asked Mom once why we never went there and she said, "That's the last place on earth I'll ever go."

I understand it's kind of crazy with all the bombings and terrorism, and I never really figured out why her parents moved there in the first place. It just seems weird not to see your grandparents.

Grandma was the only one of us holding life together. She actually made sure we ate breakfast before we left the house — not that I saw the point of that either since we ended up eating all day long at Aunt Deborah's. One night, she even drove to the WaWa corner market to buy toothpaste and tissues when she saw Mom try to blow her nose with a piece of scrap paper.

My room was messier than usual. Dirty clothes completely covered the carpet, and my mouse Morrison's cage desperately needed to be cleaned. Kleenexes overflowed my wastebasket like a gross waterfall. My room had officially turned into a pigsty.

* * * *

At breakfast the next morning, Grandma announced she wasn't going to go to Aunt Deborah's, but was staying behind to do laundry and clean the house. That's how cool she was: she could say, "No, I'm not going," and get away with it. I tried my best I'm-a-responsible-grown-up begging act on Mom so I could stay and help Grandma, but the answer was no before I could even finish my argument.

The day dragged on and I spent most of it alone in the woods, thinking about reincarnation and wondering why the hell none of us have any idea what really happens after we die, or why we're even here to begin with.

The boredom and self-imposed solitude was finally broken when Aunt Deborah found me in the yard and told me to come back to the house because Brandon had come over. Unfortunately, he wasn't alone.

"Hi, Kit. It's so good to see you," Crissy said, reaching out for a hug. "I wanted to be sure to come by tonight because I leave for Europe in the morning. I'll be gone all summer. My folks are making me go to a music camp in Switzerland." She rolled her eyes and batted them at Brandon in total Melissa fashion, over-mascaraed eyes and all.

As much as she bugged the crap out of me, Crissy did have an amazing voice and could play like five different instruments. I could barely play the piano, even after years of lessons. She had talent and money. She wouldn't be staying in this town for long.

"I wish you could stay," Brandon whispered, kissing her on the forehead.

"So, what's been going on at school?" I asked as a way to end the kissy session. We walked onto Aunt Deborah's back porch. There was a storm rolling in and the dark clouds made the sky seem like it was bedtime instead of dinnertime.

"Stuff," said Brandon, "Yesterday, there was a whole school assembly in Tyler's honor. Melissa insisted on it and read one of the poems he wrote for her."

Not surprising. Melissa had a way of assuring that the spotlight was always on her.

"A bunch of guys from track said stuff about Tyler," Brandon continued. "Coach Cline told the crowd about how Tyler always tried to include everyone and made everyone feel like they were a part of the team. He said Tyler was the ultimate team player because he hated to see anyone left out or feel alone."

While Brandon talked, my mind flashed to a time at summer camp when Tyler and I were kids. One of the counselors started a game of kickball and everyone was picking sides. There was this kid named Timmy who was a little on the porky side with thick glasses and absolutely no hand-eye coordination. Everyone was avoiding picking him for their team. Then, in such a Tyler move, Tyler stepped off his team and back into the lineup, saying that anybody who wanted him would have to take Timmy, too. The counselor was stunned. We all were.

"There wasn't a dry eye in the place," I heard Brandon say and realized I'd missed some of what he said. "The best part was when Principal DeMato let Atlantic Attack play a song for Tyler." Atlantic Attack was the coolest band at our school. It was a bunch of band and theater kids. The lead guitarist was a girl named Anna who'd wear a punked-out wig, four-inch stilettos, and her old Catholic school uniform from when she used to go to Holy Trinity. She was one of those girls I thought would be amazing to hang out with, but she was part of a crowd I never knew how to enter. There were always rumors flying about who she was hooking up with in the band. If I were her, I'd date Matthew, the lead singer.

Brandon and Crissy told me how Atlantic Attack had learned to play Break on Through by The Doors in honor of Tyler. It amazed me how many people knew Tyler's obsession with The Doors. Dad had rented the movie about Jim Morrison when we were eleven. It haunted Tyler.

Brandon and Crissy went on about life at Atlantic City High School, but it all felt so far removed from my reality. I was jealous that I wasn't there at Tyler's assembly, yet I couldn't imagine seeing all of those people and having their pity poured onto me like my relatives had been doing since the funeral.

Crissy's mom picked her up around six so she could go home to pack. I was relieved that I would have Brandon to myself for the summer. For the first time, I wondered how our relationship would be different without Crissy and Tyler around.

Brandon came home with us that night because Dad had asked him to help finish a project he and Tyler had started out in the garage a few months ago. Dad actually seemed excited that Brandon was coming over. He wouldn't stop talking the whole way home about electrical stuff and plumbing. I hadn't seen him that alive since Tyler died.

"Are you guys building an ark?"

"Cute, Kit," Dad smirked in the rearview mirror. "It's guy stuff, eh, Brandon?"

Dad didn't want me around. He wanted his son. "Yeah, I'm just a silly girl," I mumbled under my breath.

"Don't be so sensitive. You're not a silly girl, you're my girl," Dad smiled, but he was looking more at Brandon than at me.

Brandon shrugged his shoulders and looked out the window. It must have been awkward to be so intimately involved in our family drama.

Mom had fallen asleep in the front seat. Dad and Brandon continued on about their mystery project, and both made a run for the garage as soon as we pulled into the driveway.

Inside the house, Grandma Carlin was sitting at the kitchen table sorting through our mail. She was wearing a green gauzy sundress and the bright orange headband with pink and yellow flowers she usually had on. I pictured her washing clothes and dancing with the vacuum while we were sitting shiva. There was a CD case next to the stereo. Disco. I poured myself a glass of lemonade in the sparking-clean kitchen. She must have scrubbed it from floor to ceiling. And bonus! It no longer smelled like rotting garbage! Lemonade in hand, I joined her at the table to help her sort through the junk mail.

Around 10:30, I could hear Brandon saying goodbye to Dad. His dad was honking the horn in our driveway.

"Thanks, Mr. Carlin. I'll see you tomorrow night. And I can come by on Sunday if you want help with the lawn and the edging."

"Bye!" I screamed from the living room window.

"Bye, Kit!" he called back.

After Brandon left, I dropped in on Dad in the garage. Even though it was only mid-June, it was already miserably hot. The garage had poor ventilation, so was always stuffy and warm, and tonight was no exception. I walked past Tyler's boogie board and sighed.

Dad didn't hear me until I was right next to him.

"Oh! Hey sport, what do you need?" he asked without looking up from the piece of wood he was measuring.

"You know, I can mow the lawn, too. I did it a few times when Tyler broke his wrist last summer, remember?" I offered, leaning on the workbench, mindlessly twirling a screwdriver as if it were a toy top.

"That's okay. Brandon's all set to do it. We're gonna break in those jet skis Ted just bought. I told him if he could

32

come by early and help me out with a few things, then we would have more time out on the water."

"Can I come, too?"

"There won't be room. Ted's got his son, and I'll have Brandon." Dad still hadn't made eye contact.

"Oh," was all I could muster and began to walk back in the house.

"Why don't you go see if your mother needs any help? I need to finish some things out here," Dad called.

I slammed the garage door behind me and went straight to my room.

Chapter Three

It was getting to be lunchtime on day five of shiva, and I figured I should head back to the house and join the family. On my way into the yard, I overheard my parents arguing with some relatives. I followed a path around the side of the house so I could hide under the porch, slipping between a gap in the lattice work. Not able to fully stand, I leaned forward and tilted my head to the side, aiming my right ear up in order to hear more, a trick Ari, Tyler, and I used to use to spy on the adults. Usually the conversations were boring, and we'd run away in a cackling giggle, falling over each other thinking we'd been so sneaky.

"We think we've got an airtight case," Mom said.

"But I don't know that it will hold up in court." The voice sounded like Mom's cousin, Linda, who was a big-time lawyer in Philly, and everyone in the family went to her for legal advice.

"Susan, I know you don't want to hear this, but you need to come to grips with the fact that a big part of this was Tyler's fault."

"He was a child! He was my child! I want that asshole to spend the rest of his life in jail! Let him rot as he thinks about what he's done to me, to this family!" Mom screamed like she was on the verge of going nuts. My stomach turned and puke crept up into my throat.

Something made a loud crashing sound. Through the slits in the floor, it looked like Mom had thrown something, but no one said a word. I could make out a planter in pieces at the far corner of the deck.

"We're not doing this," Dad said.

"Excuse me? We've already discussed this," Mom insisted.

"Well, I changed my mind. Linda's right."

"The facts are clear," Linda began. "Tyler didn't have reflectors on his bike. With him dressed in black and riding a bike at night, how was the man to have seen him? On a blind corner like that? The driver even stayed to help. I'm sorry, but he isn't at fault here."

"So now it's Tyler fault that he got killed?" Mom's sarcasm was cutting.

"I don't want to sound like the driver's advocate but it won't stand up in court. I'm trying to stop you from an agonizing experience. You won't find the satisfaction you're seeking," Linda said.

"I'm going to find a way to get him," Mom said. "With or without your help, Jeff. That man is going to jail! He killed my baby, he killed my ba... " Her voice trailed off into sobs.

I heard the back door open and knew it was Mom who had left the porch.

Slinking my way out of the lattice, I walked back to the hammock and leaned back in. I probably would have been better off staying in it all week.

Around three o'clock, Aunt Deborah's shrink, Dr. Louise Weinstein, dropped by for an introduction. Mom and Dad knew she was coming, but somehow forgot to tell me. Figures. They didn't seem to remember me much at all anymore, especially Dad.

Dr. Weinstein was very tall, very thin, and spoke in a slow, drawn-out tone that made me feel like I was three years

35

old. Everything about her was elongated, like she was made of Silly Putty and someone had molded every detail from her long nose to her long fingers to her pointy, elf-like ears. Her fingers motioned her words like a conductor's.

It was only a fifteen-minute get-to-know-you session, but it felt like it would never end. I guess it was sort of an interview to see if we liked her and if she felt she could help us. If we all got along, then we would have an actual session in her office in Somers Point.

Apparently, Dr. Weinstein and Aunt Deborah knew each other from Temple. The thought crossed my mind that I'd never met anyone Aunt Deborah knew who she didn't meet at Temple or at the Jewish Community Center. Did she allow herself to talk to non-Jews? Mom used to tell us that she and Aunt Deborah weren't allowed to have non-Jewish friends when they were kids. They couldn't even drive a Volkswagen.

Most of my relatives still have grudges left over from World War II and the Germans. Mom said that marrying Dad was the biggest act of rebellion in her life because Dad's family was English and Scottish — and definitely not Jewish. I guess it was okay with her mom and dad because the English were our biggest ally during the war, but Mom has said that they never got over the fact that Dad didn't convert to Judaism.

Dr. Weinstein started the conversation by telling us her background almost making it sound like we should feel honored to have her to guide us through this tragic period. She fed us some long story about how her specialty was family practice and "making healthy families out of fragmented pieces." I imagined our family shattered like an expensive vase. Even if you Super-Glued it back together, the cracks would always show.

She went on: "This will be a ... very emotionally ... challenging time for you." Well, duh. I just lost my brother,

36

and very likely, my parents. I'd figured that one out on my own.

She insisted that family therapy was no place to be formal and when I called her Dr. Weinstein, she directed me to call her Louise.

Louise had us each tell stories about Tyler. What was our favorite thing about him? What would we remember most? I thought therapy sessions were one-on-one. I shifted uncomfortably in my seat and let my eyes wander the room. She was only going to get a limited amount of information out of me if Mom and Dad were in the room.

Louise never stopped smiling as she asked her questions and even her smile annoyed me. Everything was so perfect in the world she was painting, like after a few sessions together we'd forget that Tyler had died, and we'd go back to being a happy family again. Between sobs, Mom said she loved his willingness to help and how he never complained about doing chores or running errands. Of course, I was still here to do chores and run errands, but not with the superman cape that my brother wore.

Dad said he would miss sailing together. Then he said, "God only takes the good ones." Well hell, what did that make me?

Running away suddenly seemed like a damn fine idea. Maybe Tyler got the better end of the deal after all. I told them that I'd miss Tyler because he was the only person who would listen to me. I was alone now, and I told them that.

Louise said something about me being in shock and that's why I was calmer than Mom and Dad. Apparently, I was repressing feelings, which was just bull because I'd been crying so much that I thought I might need a fluid transfusion. What did she know? She had just met us. And why was our "family conversation" being run by a complete stranger anyway?

Mom fell in love with Louise immediately, much to my dismay. She and Louise agreed that Sunday night would be our scheduled time to meet with her as a family. Mom would go by herself on Wednesdays. I fought hard to make it a different night, so I could be with Brandon's family on Sunday nights, but Mom insisted that Sunday was now our "family night."

Every Sunday, Brandon's family visited their grandfather who lived in Seaside Nursing Home. Sometimes Tyler and I would go with him. It wasn't the trip to the nursing home so much as the guaranteed custard and sometimes side trip to Steel Pier to catch a few rides afterward that kept me and Tyler going.

But now that my brother had died, my family realized we needed our own family night. I bet ours wouldn't involve custard and rides.

After Louise left, friends and co-workers of my parents came by to pay their final respects. Mom was expected back at the women's clinic, where she worked as a receptionist, and Dad needed to get back to his boat shop. His buddy Ted had been covering things since the accident, but I heard Dad mention a few times that sales had been sliding since he'd been out. Summer was his busiest time of the year. In fact, I couldn't remember a single time Dad ever took off work during the summer. If he didn't go back soon, it would make things hard on us over the winter.

Besides, we all knew he'd be happier at work than here without Tyler.

Shiva finally ended after dinner, and I never wanted to see any of my Jewish relatives again, especially Aunt Deborah and Uncle David. I made a vow to myself that if I ever got married, I would elope.

Chapter Four

It was Father's Day. I decided last week that I wouldn't bring it up, and hopefully no one else would remember it either. The last thing I needed was another reminder from Dad about how he'd lost his perfect son, the child he loved most. It seemed the only thing we had in common anymore was that we were both opposed to this crazy lawsuit. When Mom wasn't zoning out in front of the TV, she was on the Internet researching cases similar to Tyler's in hopes of finding compelling arguments to convince Linda we should move forward with the case. It was like she had two gears: spacey or vengeful, neither of which were appealing. I kept hoping loving Mom would return but the glimpses were few and far between.

But getting back to Father's Day, or the ignorance of said holiday, hopefully everyone was too worked up about going to our first real visit with Louise to notice.

At breakfast, Mom and Dad were doing that super annoying parent thing where they talked about me as if I wasn't there.

"So, when does Kit start her job?" Dad asked.

"In another week," Mom answered, mindlessly flipping through the morning paper.

"Does she have everything she needs?"

"We'll go shopping before she starts and see that she does."

"Can I come?" I asked with a snide tone. They both stared at me and continued talking. In conversations, I heard them refer to "the twins" as though we were something of the past. "We used to do this or that when we had the twins," or "The twins always loved Wildwood in the summer."

"Maybe I could go spend the summer with Grandma in Florida," I suggested before scooping a spoonful of Cheerios into my mouth. Despite the brutal heat, spending the summer in Florida would be far better than having to spend another minute in this house.

"No," Dad snapped. Mom wouldn't lift her eyes from the newspaper. Over the past week, she'd developed a habit of running out to get the morning paper, turning straight to the obituaries, and calling the family of anyone who had lost a child. She would tell them all about Tyler: the accident, everything. Her frantic calls were getting really embarrassing and, quite frankly, really strange. I couldn't see how this was helping at all, and I was quite sure Louise the Shrink wouldn't approve.

"Why can't I go to Florida?" I pressed.

"No means no," Dad said as he left his dirty dish on the table and walked into the garage.

"You have your job, honey," Mom reminded me.

"They can replace me. I'm only a counselor-in-training."

"No," Mom said, but this time she took my hand and squeezed it, and between the spacey and vengeful, I got a glimpse of Don't leave me.

I squeezed her hand, smiled, and took my empty bowl and Dad's plate into the kitchen.

I'd never been to a psychologist's office before. I'm not sure if I actually expected to see one of those half-chair/half-couch thingies, in weathered paisley with gold tacks running up and down the sides. I was sure I would have to be alone at some point, and she would tell me to lie down and relax, which of course I wouldn't do. What I didn't expect was a room that looked like our living room, only much cleaner. And newer. There were two plush light-blue couches that faced one another and a nautilus shell-shaped coffee table in between. A box of Kleenex taunted me from the sparkling table.

The walls were the same mellow blue with a deeper shade sponged on top. Mom and I attempted to sponge paint our living room once but it turned out so horribly splotched we had to start over with one tone. Louise's office had an overall relaxing feel. A ceiling fan droned on above. I could almost take a nap.

Louise wore a long, flowing, silk dress and escorted us in. Tyler would have thought she was beautiful. Both of my parents sat down on one of the couches, leaving me the other to share with Louise. Wasn't she supposed to sit behind a desk?

"Have you been in therapy before, Katrina?" she asked.

"It's Kit," I sighed as I edged away from her and closer to the arm of the couch.

"Oh! Thank you for correcting me."

"No, I've never been to therapy." And I don't want to be here now, I thought to myself. I started picking at my hair and looking for split ends to pull apart. Normally, Mom yelled at me when I did that, but I glanced her way and she was fixed on Louise.

"Well, I'm sure you've heard many different stories about what goes on in a psychologist's office. Hopefully, this will be a rewarding experience, and one that will assist you in handling your grief."

"I'm doing fine," I mumbled under my breath.

"Kit!" Dad yelled. I rolled my eyes and looked out the window. It seemed like I couldn't do anything these days without getting a snap and stare from Dad.

41

"Kit," Louise let out a long sigh then let silence hang in the air for a moment. "Tell me about how you've been doing lately. Have you had any upsetting dreams for instance?"

"No."

"What about the one earlier this week?" Mom interjected, and I shot her the evil-eye glare she sometimes gave me.

"I don't want to go into it," I growled.

"That's okay. I'm here to help."

"Honey, I really want you to share it with Louise. That's why we're here." Any time Mom said honey, she got me. It was like I was a baby again and totally cradled and held in her love.

Louise's manicured fingernails fell lightly on my leg and sent goose bumps up my spine. I was wearing shorts because of the heat, but suddenly wished I had opted for jeans.

"Okay, I had a nightmare last night." I tried to leave it at that, but everyone kept staring. "I dreamt that I was swimming out past the breakers and I was all alone. It was peaceful and calm. Tyler hovered just before the horizon, so I kept swimming faster and faster to catch him. The next thing I knew, a gigantic tidal wave came out of nowhere. I tried to make my way back to shore, but the undertow kept getting stronger and stronger. I had swum out too far to make it back. I started to go under the wave. Then I woke up."

"Thank you, Kit. It took a lot of courage to share that." Louise sipped her mineral water before continuing. "Tonight, I'd like you to write down three things that make you different from Tyler. Then I want you to meditate on these things before you fall asleep. We'll go over some meditation techniques before you leave."

"Yeah, right," I muttered.

Mom raised her eyebrows at me and Dad started fidgeting. He didn't want to be here. I overheard him and Mom fighting about it last night. He said that we'd get over it in time, but Mom told him she didn't think she could do it on her own. Mom's been really weird since everything happened, like she can't quite seem to wake up all the way. I think she's still on the Valium her doctor prescribed the night of the accident.

"The longer you fight it, the harder it will be to get through the grieving process and move on to a healing path," Louise said. "I think you can handle this."

"Did you know we're Geminis? That's the sign of the twins. Our birthday was five days before he died."

"I didn't know that. How interesting. Do you follow astrology?"

"A little."

"Tell me what you know of Gemini."

"Oh, please! This is costing me a fortune," Dad sighed. "What does that have to do with Tyler?"

"Mr. Carlin, I'm just trying to get to know you all a little better." Louise politely put Dad in his place, and I had to admit I was quite impressed. "Please continue," she insisted and laid her hand on my knee for the second time.

"Umm, I can't remember the question." I started picking at my hair again.

"What do you know of the sign of Gemini?" Louise repeated.

"Umm ... ." I couldn't get my head straight to talk while Dad sat there with his arms crossed, staring at Louise. I wanted to point out to her that this is the real reason we should be in therapy: that Dad could be such a jerk sometimes. Women's lib means nothing to him, and boys are better than girls, and everything was tolerable until Tyler died, but now that Dad didn't have a son, he was taking it out on me.

I guess Louise could tell I wasn't going to talk any time soon, so she released me and turned her attention to Dad. "Now, Jeff, what steps have you initiated on your own to cope with Tyler's absence?"

"Alcohol," I blurted. Dad flushed red, and I knew I had gone too far.

"I'm done!" Dad yelled at Mom. Mom had a blank look on her face like everything was just too much to handle. I was speechless and looked to Louise for help. Can't someone fix our family?

"Kit? Susan? Could you wait in the lobby? I'd like to speak with Jeff alone."

I jumped off the couch and bolted for the door, happy to leave Dad with Louise. Mom followed, although she kept looking back over her shoulder. I wished she would drive us home and leave Dad here. He could hitchhike back for all I cared. About twenty minutes passed during which I flipped through boring magazines like Reader's Digest and Sunset. Dad finally emerged, but all he said was that it was time to go. Louise bowed goodbye to us, and we drove home in complete silence.

When we got back to the house, Dad headed straight for the garage and Mom for the kitchen where she set about cutting up pieces of leftover key lime pie as if it were the most important task she could find. Key lime pie was my favorite dessert, especially with lots of whipped cream, but I had no appetite. When Mom, Grandma, and I sat down at the table, Grandma announced she'd booked her reservation and needed a ride to the train station first thing in the morning.

"I thought you were staying for a few weeks!" I said.

"It's time for you all to move on without me," she said, her gaze focused on her pie, avoiding Mom.

"What happened?" I demanded of Mom.

"Nothing, honey. Grandma needs to go," Mom said in her You're just a kid voice that pissed me off even more.

"No! Something happened." I dropped my fork onto my plate and pushed it away. "Did you guys get in a fight?"

"Nothing happened," Grandma said, reaching out to hold my hand, but I pulled it away. "I have my own life in Florida," she said. "It's time for me to get back to it. My neighbor, Gracie, has probably clear knocked me off the shuffleboard circuit."

I could tell she was only pretending. Something had happened. "It was Dad, wasn't it?"

"Kit ..."

"Dad did something stupid, didn't he?" I pushed my chair away and stood up, my whole body shaking. Dad was the one who needed to be sent away. "I want to go to Florida with Grandma for the summer," I demanded.

Mom kept eating her pie and refused to make eye contact.

"Maybe you can come for a visit," Grandma said as she took her plate into the kitchen.

I kept staring at Mom.

"We'll see," Mom said, which meant no.

I grabbed my plate, stomped into the kitchen, and dumped my dessert into the trash.

I was sulking in my room, plotting how best to run away, when Grandma tapped on the door.

"Can I come in?" She slowly opened the door.

"Sure," I shrugged and rolled over making enough room for her to sit on the edge of my bed.

"Listen, I know it's been tough around here, kiddo, especially with your Dad, but they really do need you here. I know sometimes it feels like they've forgotten about you. With Tyler gone, honey, you're all they have."

That wasn't very reassuring.

She reached for my hand and placed it between her palms, squeezing it tight. "Doll, I'd love to have you with me in Florida. I know we'd have a grand ol' time, but maybe next summer. Right now, the shock of you gone would tear them apart."

"I'm sick of being either ignored or yelled at. Dad makes me feel like he wished I'd died instead. I hate being here. I hated being at Aunt Deborah's. I just need to get out of New Jersey. I don't belong anymore. Not without Tyler," I said, then blew a mucousy mess into a tissue.

"Oh sweetie, don't say such things."

"But it's true. I can feel it. I'm not dumb."

"No one ever said you were. Your father loves you so very much."

I rolled my eyes.

"He'll come around. This grief is way too unbearable for him, your mother, too. They're each figuring out their own ways to process and cope, just like you."

"What happened with Dad?" I begged. "Please tell me."

"He needs you all to move on with your life, and having me here doesn't help. I love your Dad very much, but we get along better when we're not in the same house."

"Me, too," I smiled.

"It's time for me to go."

"I'm going to miss you," I said as tears welled in my eyes.

"I'm just a phone call away," she reassured me as she smiled and squeezed my hand.

✳ ✳ ✳ ✳

I had to walk by Tyler's bedroom to get to my own, and the ache I felt passing his door grew in intensity each night. Mom would freak if she saw his door open. But I was determined to go in there soon, maybe when everyone was asleep. I mindlessly started moving the clean piles of clothes Grandma had left on my bed into my dresser drawers.

The house was scary quiet, and I couldn't handle it anymore. I cued up my Doors playlist on my phone and inserted my ear buds. It was the first time I'd listened to The

Doors since Tyler died. Tears were streaming down my face as Jim Morrison's voice filled my ears. I started to move to the music, using the clothes like scarves, pretending I was Stevie Nicks in her flowing gypsy outfit from the concert video of Fleetwood Mac that Mom and I used to watch when I was a kid.

"This is the end. My only friend, the end," Jim Morrison belted out his famous line and I cranked up the volume as loud as my ears could take it until my tears felt like the music, cleaning me from the inside out.

Chapter Five

Mom took Grandma to the train station on her way to work. By 8:30, the house was empty and I set about my day of nothingness.

I'd taken a job as a counselor-in-training at the Jewish Community Center's Camp by the Sea for the summer. My house was blocks from the JCC, so I didn't have to rely on Mom for a ride. Aunt Deborah got me the job because she was on the board of directors. It was one of the few times I didn't mind Aunt Deborah butting into my life.

Tyler and I had spent tons of summers at the JCC camp as kids, and it was always a dream of mine to work there as a counselor, especially to teach gymnastics. While I was at camp, Tyler was supposed to work in Dad's boat shop like he had the last few summers, learning "the family business." He was already good at telling the difference between different types of boat motors, and he was getting pretty handy at helping Dad with the boat repair side of the business. Now, Dad had to scramble to hire someone. What a sucky job that would be: "I'm here to replace the owner's dead son."

School had been out for a few weeks now and camp was a week away, so I hunkered down on the couch and lost myself in stupid TV shows.

It was the first day I'd been alone in the house since everything happened, and I decided to venture into Tyler's room. My heart pounded as I twisted the doorknob. I jumped out of my skin when I heard the neighbors' car pull up in front of their house and reminded myself over and over that Mom and Dad wouldn't be home for hours. They never came home randomly in the middle of the day; plus, Mom had a meeting with Linda over her lunch break, and she certainly wasn't going to miss that.

The windows were closed and the curtains shut, so if I pretended, I could believe that Tyler was just sleeping in late under the mess of covers on the bed. Dirty clothes were scattered across the floor and the room flat-out stank. His track trophies were slowly gathering dust.

I looked around the room, taking everything in. I was amazed at the amount of junk Tyler had collected over the years. When I saw his poster of The Doors on the back of his door, signed by Ray Manzarek, the band's keyboardist, I started to cry.

We had gone to Philly to meet Ray at an in-store music event. On the way, we got a flat tire; a totally crazy story about having to change the spare on the side of the highway, but then we got to the store right as they were closing. Tyler ran across the parking lot screaming "Ray!" with his poster gripped firmly in his hand like the baton in a relay race. The good sprinter that he was, Tyler was able to stop Ray as he was backing out of his parking space. Ray signed the poster on the roof of his rental car while listening to our sob story about the flat tire and the trek down the highway to three different gas stations trying to find a spare. Tyler really laid on his love of The Doors. After finding out that we hadn't eaten dinner, and obviously impressed with Tyler's adoration, Ray invited us to join him to eat. We couldn't believe it. We actually got to eat dinner with Ray Manzarek!

Ray was impressed with Tyler's poetry and lyrics, even saying how he reminded him a little of Jim Morrison. He asked Tyler to mail him some of his songs. They wrote back and forth for a good six months before Ray stopped writing. I wondered if I should write Ray and tell him what happened. Maybe he'd publish Tyler's lyrics and make him famous.

Some schoolbooks and the beginnings of a homework assignment for Algebra were on his beanbag. I moved them and sat down. The algebra book fell open in my lap and out popped a birthday card. It was from Melissa. I felt guilty reading it, but couldn't stop myself.

My T. Bear,
Hope this year brings ALL that your heart desires.
Lots o' love –
Your M. Doll

I could hear the phone ringing, but I just sat there, unable to move. Our birthday. Just a few weeks ago. Mom and Dad had surprised us with Phillies tickets. The night was simply perfect. The Phillies were on fire and blew out the San Diego Padres. Tyler even caught a foul ball. As I closed my eyes, I pictured Mom and Dad smiling, Tyler and my epic search for a soft pretzel after the seventh-inning stretch. His last game. His last birthday. Next year, I'll turn sixteen and he'll be forever locked in time.

Ten minutes or an hour later – I had no idea how long I'd been sitting — I grabbed Tyler's iPod and some books and moved them to my room. After I moved a second stack of books, a notebook I'd never seen fell off his bookshelf. The front of the book read:

Mosaic: a series of notes, prose-poems, stories, bits of plays & dialogue. Aphorisms, epigrams, essays. Poems? Sure.
— Jim Morrison

It was full of song lyrics he'd jotted down from a bunch of different bands and singers. I read for a while before I noticed the pages were getting wet from my tears. The last half of the book was empty. Something in me picked up a pen lying on the floor and began writing in the date:

50

June 22nd
Dear Tyler,
How are you doing? Are you happy? Have you run into Jim Morrison? What I really want to know is, where are you?

I laughed. This was so ridiculous. But I kept writing.

I think about you all the time, especially at night when the house is quiet and my thoughts take over. Life is pretty strange around here. I get mad at myself a lot because I can't stop crying. I keep wondering if there was a way I could have stopped everything. If Dad had given you a ride home that night, or if you had stayed overnight at Brandon's instead of riding your bike home, could we have stopped this from happening? I still haven't told anyone about that dream I had, not even Louise, this therapist we have to go see.
You remember it, don't you? In the dream, you and I were trapped in a building that was filling with smoke. Our oxygen was running out and the door was jammed shut. It was getting so bad inside that we were lying on the ground, choking, barely able to get out our last words. You told me how you felt bound to me, that we were reflections of each other on the inside, as well as the out,

which was really weird but also kinda cool. I told you that I understood who you really were, although I'm still not sure what that meant. As you were dying, you told me that we would meet again in a happier place and that we would never be apart. When I told you about it, you laughed and said it was only a bad dream. Two weeks later, you were dead.

Mom has lost it. She cries all the time and watches endless amounts of reality TV and game shows. Well, I guess I have been, too. But whenever I try to talk to her, I know she can hear my voice, but what I'm saying just drifts right through one ear and out the other, totally bypassing her brain.

Dad just wants you back. I always knew he liked you best. It's like you died, and with you went the twins, and now he's surprised to find he still has a daughter. Basically, it sucks. Lately, I've been so mad at you for leaving, but then I feel guilty because it wasn't like you wanted to go. I wish I could have gone with you. No one ever told me that I might have to live without my twin someday. Louise says my feelings are normal. I don't feel very normal.

Brandon's about to leave for California to visit his uncle and I wish I could make him stay. I know *it's a little over a week, but he's the only person who keeps me from feeling completely alone. I guess he's handling this all pretty well. I only saw him cry the day of the funeral. Don't tell him I told you.*

Melissa still has your class ring. I told Brandon to get it back from her, but he hasn't yet. He probably won't because he thinks you want her to have it. If I had it, I would wear it like a pendant around my neck.

Well, I should probably go. I'm scared out of my mind that Mom or Dad are going to come home and find me here in your room. I promise I'll write more soon. I wish you were here. I miss you. Damn, I miss you so much.

Love,

your sis, K

I hid the journal under Tyler's bed and shut the door behind me.

In a daze, I floated downstairs. I was mildly hungry, but as I stared at the open fridge, I couldn't summon the energy to actually make something, so I grabbed a cheese stick and a handful of grapes. My phone chimed with a text from Brandon.

"Packing done! Come swim."

"Be right there!" I wrote back.

Swimming sounded so normal. That's what I needed to do. Go to Brandon's and swim. I raced back upstairs, put on my suit, threw on one of Dad's old T-shirt's from his shop and a pair of jean shorts, and whipped my hair into a low ponytail.

I barely remembered to slip on my flip-flops as I wheeled my bike out of the garage. I was a good three blocks from home before I realized that it was the first bike ride since Tyler died. Then my legs turned shaky and I began meandering back and forth rather than riding in a straight line. "Get yourself together, girl," I scolded myself as I stopped in someone's driveway, leaned my head forward, and attempted some deep Grandma-yoga-style breathing. With the breath came tears. Tears for what? Who knows? A huge mess is what I'd turned into. Frustrated, I wiped them away, sat back on the bike seat and peddled toward Brandon's house.

When I rounded a corner, a car came racing behind me, catching me off-guard. I fell to the curb and scrapped my knee. I took a leaf off a tree and wiped away the blood. What would happen if I died too? Is that my fate? Jeez, I needed help! I stopped the bleeding, hopped back on my bike, and didn't stop peddling until I reached Brandon's.

Brandon was already in the pool when I got there.

"Hey there!" I called as I opened the gate to the backyard.

"Come on in!" he called back.

"First I need a Band-Aid," I said, pointing to my knee.

"There's a first-aid kit over there, in that cabinet." Brandon pointed to the other side of the deck where the pool toys and deck gear were kept. I selected a Thomas the Tank Engine Band-Aid and giggled.

"Not used too often, eh? Or are these your brother's?"

"They're Jason's, although even he isn't into Thomas anymore. They're old."

I walked back to the pool and removed my T-shirt and shorts. Standing in just my bathing suit alone with Brandon, I was oddly aware that this was the first time Brandon and I had been alone in his pool. No Melissa, Crissy, or Tyler, just us. I searched Brandon's face for any signs that this was unusual, but he just started taunting me that I couldn't catch him, and I screamed "Heads up!" before I cannonballed right next to him.

My cut knee stung, but oddly it was an amazing reminder that I was alive. My arms moved in circles and my legs powered through the sting.

"God, this feels so good!" I exhaled as I surfaced, leaning my head back and letting the water drain off my face and down my hair.

"I know! This summer has been so hot. I've been in here multiple times a day. My uncle has a totally killer pool with a diving board and attached hot tub. I'll be in that every day. You know, 'swim team practice.'"

"Right, and you're not even on the swim team."

"Well, there's always next year," he said and climbed out of the pool.

"I can't believe you're leaving tonight. I'm so jealous. I wish I could go with you. How long are you going to be gone again?"

"Ten days. I'll send a postcard."

"Ooh, old school! Bring me a cheesy souvenir, too!"

"Of course. Maybe a snow globe from Universal Studios?"

"Man, are you sure you don't have room for me in your suitcase?"

Brandon laughed and cannonballed right next to me.

"Okay, yes, a snow globe sounds perfect! Do that!" I said as I wiped the water from his cannonball splash away from my eyes.

Every year, Brandon would bring back stuff for Tyler and me from his trip to California. My favorite was the surfer girl snow globe that said Huntington Beach, which of course made no sense. Why would there be snow while you're surfing?

Tyler and I never traveled much. One jaunt to Disneyworld in Florida on the way to see Grandma was the highlight of our travels. With Dad's business, summertime meant long, crazy hours in the shop, not vacation time.

I was already fantasizing about going to college out of state — just to experience something other than New Jersey. California sounded like a dream. I pictured hanging on Venice Beach like Jim Morrison, people-watching the hippies and the punks. I could go for a major life overhaul. I should start researching UCLA. Then again, I could head to Miami and be near Grandma. I just needed to get away from here. I'd better not end up at Rutgers.

"What am I going to do without you for ten days? That's practically two weeks!" I whined as I treaded water in the deep end and watched Brandon climb out of the pool and prepare for another dive.

"Oh, you'll survive. When does camp start?"

"Right about when you come home."

"Heads up!" he called as he crashed into the water again.

"I keep watching soap operas. You know, they might really start pulling me in," I warned after he surfaced.

"No!" he fake cried as he swam toward me.

"I know. I'm falling into the stereotype of a teenage girl," I laughed, tossing the back of my hand over my forehead in a mock faint.

"Not my Kit!"

"Oh, save me, Brandon! Don't let my perfect hairdo get a drop of water on it! Oh, and my mascara will run!"

We were both laughing like crazy as he swam closer and placed his arms under my torso in a pretend save. When we finally calmed down, his arms were still holding me and he was looking me in the eyes. It was awkward, but also a little nice. Then Brandon laughed and dunked me.

"You're one girl who does not need saving," he said when I came up for air. I'm sure he meant it as a compliment, but it didn't feel like one.

"So has Crissy left for Europe?"

"Yeah. She took off a few days ago. It's weird to think she'll be gone all summer." And really terrific, I thought, but I didn't say it.

"You'll just have to suffer with me."

"Okay. If I have to," he mocked and then swam down to the shallow end.

It was a good hour or more before Brandon and I got out of the pool. Mrs. Gardner in all of her mom lovingness brought out lemonade and cookies for us. I needed to find a way to get adopted by her.

When the swimming was over, I realized I'd completely spaced bringing underwear and a bra so I either had to go without or wear my wet suit under my clothes. One of the benefits of having no boobs is that when you wear a baggy shirt, no one can really tell that you're braless. I put my wet suit in a plastic garbage bag and hung it from my bike handle.

"Okay, well you have tons of fun," I said as I gave him a hug.

"I will."

"And I'll look for your postcard."

"Don't worry, I won't forget. Crissy's asked for one every day."

My heart sank a bit at the mention of Crissy. I liked having Brandon all to myself while she was gone.

"How do you send one to Europe?"

"Yeah, not so sure on the logistics there."

"Well, I hope mine comes before you get back."

"Take care of yourself," Brandon said, hugging me a bit longer and a bit tighter than usual.

I hugged him back and nearly kissed his cheek. Instead, I gave a big smile before getting on my bike. "Send me pictures, too!" I called back before turning the corner and riding home.

Chapter Six

The rest of the week went by in a blur. By Wednesday, I was addicted to five new TV shows, and could barely summon the energy to make lunch or leave the house. When I wasn't zombified in front of the TV, I spent the rest of the week at the beach, listening to The Doors over and over on my phone.

The Saturday before camp began, Mom and I headed out to Hamilton Mall. I needed to find a new gymnastics leotard, bathing suit, and other summer necessities, like sunglasses and sunscreen.

"Kit, look at this T-shirt. Wouldn't Tyler have loved it?"

I peeked into the store window past Mom and saw a faded black and grey shirt with The Doors' first album cover on the front.

"Yeah, that's pretty cool. He definitely would have liked it," I said in a wistful tone. I kept walking. After a few steps, I noticed Mom wasn't with me. When I turned back around, I saw her inside the store. I hustled back to get her.

"Mom! What are you doing?" I whispered in a scolding tone like she was the child and I was the mom. I grabbed her arm and pulled her back toward the front of the store.

"I'm going to buy that shirt," she huffed and pushed my hand off her arm.

"No, you're not!" I commanded, grabbing her wrist.

"Let go of me, Kit!" she snapped and pushed me away.

"Mom, you're embarrassing me," I hissed in her ear.

"Shush!" The two guys standing behind the counter were staring at us. "I'd like to buy that shirt in the window," Mom said, as though nothing had happened.

"Don't do this," I begged as I attempted to shrink my presence and will myself away from this crazy scene.

"I would prefer a medium if you have one, otherwise large would be fine. My son is going to love this shirt. He's a huge Doors fan."

"You don't have a son!" I screamed.

Mom stared at me, a hollowed-eye stare that left me feeling confused and abandoned. I took a step back. She turned from me, back to the counter, as if I wasn't even there.

"Let me go in the back and check," one clerk said, raising an eyebrow to the other.

Thank God neither of them looked familiar. Lots of ACHS kids worked at the mall over the summer, so the chance of running into someone I knew was pretty good. "I'll be outside," I barked as rudely as I could muster to try to get her attention, but she didn't even notice me stomping away.

Mom came out of the store a few minutes later holding a shopping bag. We walked through the mall in silence. Neither of us said a word until we got to Macy's. I walked toward the Junior Misses section, but Mom wasn't following.

"I thought we came here so I could get a bathing suit," I said, walking back to her.

"Go ahead. I want to look at some clothes down here. I'll come up in a few minutes."

I shook my head and left. What did I need her for anyway?

A half hour went by and Mom never showed. I found a hot-pink bikini, but I had to find Mom since she had the money. I stepped onto the downstairs escalator and as it brought me to the lower level, I could see her in the guys' section. At least this time she didn't appear to be buying anything. But she was stroking the jeans in a super creepy way.

"Mom, I found a suit," I said, holding up the bikini on its hanger to get her attention.

"Oh now, really, Kit!" she said, covering her mouth with her hand. "You're not buying that."

"Why not?"

"A bikini is not very practical for camp. Go pick out a sporty one-piece," she insisted, turning back to the jeans.

"I already have several one-pieces and I end up with crappy tans. Besides, no one else wears them. They make me feel like a kid ... or a mom."

"You're too young for a bikini."

"Mom, I'm 15!"

"No."

"I had one last summer. What's the big deal?"

"Fine. I'm not going to stand here all day and argue with you."

"Good," I mumbled under my breath.

"What was that?"

"Nothing. Can we go now?"

"What about shorts?"

"I'm going to cut some of my jeans off and make shorts."

"No, I'll buy you some shorts. Those cut-offs look sloppy. They're okay for your Dad on the boat but they're not for a lady."

"I like them."

"Oh, Kit. You're so impossible."

We paid for my bathing suit and then it was on to the Danskin store for a new leotard. At least there wasn't anything there that reminded her of Tyler.

On the way home, we stopped at KFC and picked up a bucket for dinner. When we got to the house, Dad still wasn't home.

"I wonder where your father is."

"You think I keep his schedule?"

"Don't give me that lip."

"Sorry," I said and I meant it. "Can we eat? I'm starving."

"Let's wait for your father."

"I'll be in my room," I sighed and walked upstairs.

An hour went by and still no Dad. I finally got so hungry I couldn't take it anymore. I went downstairs and found Mom zoned out in front of the TV watching something on The Food Network. My stomach growled.

"Mom, can I eat yet?"

"What time is it?"

"It's almost eight."

"Is it that late? I'm sorry, honey. Go ahead."

I heated up the chicken in the microwave but it came out soggy. It would have tasted fine if I could have eaten it when we got home and it was still hot. After piling on some mashed potatoes, gravy, and a biscuit, I took the plate up to my room. I wasn't supposed to take food upstairs, but nobody seemed to care about anything anymore.

An hour later, Mom knocked on my door. In the light of the hallway, the puffy bags under her eyes were even more pronounced. In the bathroom this morning, I'd noticed a newly full bottle of prescription sleeping pills. I wondered how they were reacting with the Valium she claimed she'd stopped taking. There was a brand new bottle of that in the medicine cabinet a few days ago.

"He's still not home and he's not answering his cell; I'm going to look for your father," Mom said, her purse slung over her shoulder, keys dangling from her finger, and shoulders uncharacteristically slouched forward.

"Do you want me to come?"

"No. Stay here in case he comes back. Call me if he does."

"Okay."

As soon I was sure she was gone, I went downstairs to watch TV.

Dad stumbled in about a half-hour later, tripping over the doorstep as he walked through the front door. Mom wasn't home yet.

"Boy, are you in for it," I called from the couch.

"Where's your mother?"

"She went out looking for you. Where have you been?" I turned off the terrible zombie movie I was watching and walked over to make sure Dad was okay. He didn't look good.

"I was with the guys."

I knew what that meant. "You reek of booze. You're drunk!"

"Go to your room," he said, shooing me away as he fumbled to untie his shoes.

"Mom's gonna be pissed," I said, leaning on the banister.

"Get outta here." His words slurred and he reached like he was going to push me, but I darted up the stairs.

"You know, Dad, you've been a real jerk!" The words flew out of my mouth as I sprinted up the stairs.

"You're a fucking brat!" he screamed after me.

I slammed my bedroom door and locked it as I heard him fall on the stairs. I was about to call Mom, but then her car pulled into the driveway. The front door opened and slammed.

"You asshole!" Mom yelled. "Where the hell have you been? Or should I be asking who the hell have you been with? I've been worried sick!"

"Why should I race home to deal with this crap? You could have called and found out where I was. Besides, you knew where I was."

"And apparently too busy to be bothered with answering your phone. You had no issue with the fact that your dinner was cold or that we would have actually been waiting for you to eat!"

"Oh, don't start with that crap, Susan. I'm so sick of this house. I can't breathe here anymore."

"Crap? That's what this? Your poor daughter was starving. Maybe your wife was worried. Jesus, Jeff!"

"I've had it with her! I've had it with everything."

I heard something crash. Was it the bowl that held the car keys on the front table? Their voices got more intense and Mom sounded panicked. Doors started slamming and I scrambled to unlock my bedroom door and bolted for the bathroom. Just as I made it across the hallway, I heard Dad say, "Why did my son have to be the one who died?" and I threw up all over the bathroom floor.

Chapter Seven

The next day was my first private session with Louise. Mom drove me, but waited in the lobby. I felt so unsafe and vulnerable being in Louise's office without Mom and even Dad there; although, at some level, I was happy to not be judged for what I may or may not say.

"How are you doing today?" Louise was wearing another beautiful sundress. She always looked so put together, like she was an actress in her own life.

"I'm okay." I debated whether or not to tell her about Dad and my gastro-reaction last night.

"Just okay?"

"I'm fine. What are we going to talk about today?"

She sensed I was avoiding something.

"I was going to see what you wanted to talk about. The first time we met, we had started to talk about astrology. Did you want to talk about that now?"

"Nah, I don't think we need to talk about that anymore." I could only imagine how much trouble I'd be in if Louise and I spent the whole hour talking about astrology.

"What's life been like for you the last few weeks since Tyler's been gone?"

"Strange."

"Can you expand on that?"

I shifted back and forth on the couch. I didn't know if I hated being there or if I was relieved to have someone to talk to.

"I cry at weird times." Suddenly, talking wasn't so bad. "You know, like when I'm taking out the garbage or walking by a playground we used to play at. I get really sad."

"Go on," Louise's eyes were calming and I found myself wanting to talk more than I'd planned.

"I get frustrated because I can't talk to him anymore. I can't talk to my parents either. Dad's hardly ever around and when he is, he's in the garage and too wrapped up in his stuff to notice me. Mom is either completely neurotic about something as small as how a pan got washed or she's lying on the couch, watching TV and crying." I almost started talking about all of Mom's various pills, but then decided that wouldn't be smart.

Louise nodded, so I kept going.

"It seems to me that I'm handling this better than my parents, so when I feel scared and need someone, I have no one to turn to. Mom and I used to be close, but it's like part of her died with Tyler. Sometimes I see glimpses of the old her, but mostly she's just an empty shell."

"Your mother's bearing a lot of grief, but she still loves you very much. You can always turn to me," Louise said. "Did you do the meditations on twin separation that I recommended last time?"

"No."

"I think they'll help."

"Listen, Louise, this may sound crazy, but I feel like if I do, I'll disappear, too. I know you're an expert and all, but you don't know what it's like to be a twin."

"You're right. I don't," she admitted, shocking me with her honesty. "Why don't you explain to me more about how you're feeling? I'd like to understand."

"It's like a part of me is missing." I squeaked out the last words as I reached for the box of Kleenex. I wondered how many times a week she had to put out a new box.

"It's okay to cry." Louise moved so that she was sitting on the couch next to me. I wished she wouldn't have, but I was crying too much to say anything. We sat in silence for several minutes as she held my hand. There was something so comforting about her that it made me want to open up even more. I tried to fight it, but it was like she'd put a spell on me.

"This is hard to explain, but I'm not as mad about his death as everyone else is. I have a feeling that I should feel worse than I do, that I should want the driver to die or something, but I don't."

"You don't have to feel vengeful to miss your brother," she said, reaching for her mineral water.

"I cry and I miss him. I look for him and forget he's not here. He's always been here. Always, you know? My mom's all gung-ho about seeing the driver in jail, but I don't want to hurt his family too."

"Kit, what do you think happens to someone when they die?"

Her question caught me off guard, and I sat there truly wondering. What did I believe? Is that what all of this comes down to?

"I'm not sure. I think I believe what my Grandma believes. That Tyler still exists, but he's a spirit now."

"I sense that you're very special, Kit. You seem to have a deep level of understanding of things greater than our world. You are an "old soul" as some would say, and you are much stronger than you think. Do your parents share your views?"

"Are you kidding me?"

"What do your parents believe?"

"I have no idea, but they don't believe in reincarnation."

"Have you ever asked them?"

I'd thought about having a real conversation with Dad, like we used to when I was a kid, walking on the beach collecting clam and mussel shells. That life was only a few years ago, but it felt like another incarnation, as Grandma would say.

"Maybe your sense of balance in dealing with this trauma stems from the fact that you don't see your brother as gone so much as having changed forms, we'll say. He still exists to you. Does that make sense?"

I nodded. Everything in my mind clicked into place. It was like she unlocked the missing key to solve the puzzle.

"Your parents remain in shock. To them, he's gone and that's unacceptable. They haven't let themselves think about whether or not he might still exist."

"But if my parents aren't there for me, then where do I go? I can talk to my Grandma, but she's in Florida."

"Tell me more about your relationship with your grandmother."

"She's great. She's going to send me some books on reincarnation. She's been more like me through all this, not so freaked out and mad all the time. I want to go down to Florida for the summer, but my parents won't let me. They did say that I could go next summer, though, and I'm not going to let them forget that."

"Well, then, I guess for now you'll have to get your support from conversations with your grandma. And you know that we can always have an open and honest dialogue here. Everything that's said between us is confidential. Nothing will leave this room."

I half-smiled at Louise. I didn't know how I felt about having her as my support, but this was the first real conversation I'd had about Tyler since Grandma went home. Suddenly, thoughts that were hurting my head for weeks felt lighter.

"What do you think happens to people when they die?" I turned her question on her.

"Kit, it's not professional of me to share my personal views."

"Really?"

"Yes."

"Could you break your rules for me? I don't have any other adults I can talk to about this stuff. I really feel like it would help."

"Well ..."

"Aw, come on, live a little. I won't tell," I pushed and Louise smiled and turned away. I felt like I'd finally broken through her plastic veneer and caught a glimpse of the real her.

"Okay, Kit, but only for you. My ideas are quite simple, actually. I don't believe that there is an afterlife. I believe that when you die, that's pretty much it."

"But aren't you Jewish?" I blurted out in surprise.

"Aren't you? We have faiths and belief systems — cultures that we're raised with — that support us and give us community, but sometimes that's not enough. Sometimes, we have a deeper sense of a different truth, a truth that we come to all on our own, and no matter what our religious upbringing may teach us, those truths don't ring true. Buddha had a great saying, and one I firmly encourage people to take to heart: 'Believe nothing, no matter where you read it or who has said it, not even if I have said it, unless it agrees with your own reason and your own common sense.' For you, that truth may be life after death, an existence that extends beyond this life."

"But you believe in God, right?"

"I'm not sure."

"Really? Wow."

"It's called agnosticism. You don't necessarily believe that God exists, but you don't discount it either. You simply remain open to the idea."

"That seems so ... lonely."

"For me, it makes every second on earth precious and worth its weight in gold. Perhaps we should move on to another topic. I want to be mindful of our time, and we still need to review this handout."

I didn't want to stop talking about the spiritual stuff, but I followed her lead. She reviewed a brochure with me that went into detail about the stages of grief. She wanted me to be able to recognize each stage as I went through it. I had no idea what stage I was in, but I promised I'd try to pay attention.

* * * *

Mom and I made it home around four o'clock. A storm was rolling in and the sky was growing darker. I made sure Mom was settled by the TV and told her I was going out for a bit, but that I'd be back by dinner. She didn't want me to go, so I lied and said I needed to get something at Weiss's Corner Store, and that I'd be right back.

I went into the garage and wheeled out my bike. I still sometimes got spooked riding it. My frustration mounted as my shaky hands lamely grasped the rubber handles. When I pushed my butt back to mount the seat, I lost my nerve and ended up toppling onto the driveway. I told myself I was being ridiculous. It's the same bike I'd been riding since I was eleven. I tried again and everything was fine and normal, so normal that I could imagine letting the wheels roll me somewhere far, far away.

As usual, I found myself at the beach. I loved the way the ocean looked as a storm rolled in. The waves looked so angry and everything was so intense. It made me feel like I was seeing nature when she didn't know I was looking.

I locked my bike by the boardwalk and walked for a while, aimlessly picking up broken shells. The water kept beckoning me, and the beach was desolate for miles. I took off my T-shirt and walked toward the water's edge wearing only my bra and shorts. The coolness drew me in as I waded out, my eyes fixed on the horizon. When I had waded out to thigh level, I dove under a large wave before it broke. From the ocean floor, I could hear the wave crash above. The water was still cold this early in the summer, but I didn't care. I broke the surface and the taste of the saltwater on my lips felt cleansing. I ran my tongue back and forth, soaking it in. I let the waves toss my body around, hoping they might carry me out to sea. With my eyes closed, I imagined my body disappearing. If I relaxed enough, maybe I could join Tyler and be free.

I thought about Louise's take on death. Maybe there was nothing beyond our life here after all: no heaven, no hell, no reincarnation. We come from the earth and we return to it to break down when we die. If I just let the waves take me away, I could end all my pain and suffering. A powerful wave washed over me, catching me off guard. I began to choke on the saltwater. In a panic, I caught the next wave and body surfed to shore, surprised at my instinct to survive. Back on the beach, I shook the sand off my T-shirt and slipped it on over my wet bra. The air was freezing and I was shivering from head to toe as I walked toward the boardwalk. By the time I reached my bike, rain was coming down in sheets.

Chapter Eight

Sometimes there are moments when it hits me: "Damn, Kit! You're turning into an adult." Stepping into the JCC as a counselor instead of a camper was one of those moments. I didn't feel that much older, but there I was, surrounded by other teenagers and looking at the kids, well, like they were kids.

We had to be there at 10:00 a.m. on the Friday before camp started for a pre-camp orientation. I walked into the gym to find folding chairs set up in a circle. While I'd often see adults around camp who weren't counselors, I had no idea who they were or what they did. The only person sitting in the circle had a nametag: Mrs. Meyers, Camp Director. I recognized her. She was the one I'd interviewed with, and the one who sent me the letter saying I'd gotten the job.

Mrs. Meyers was freakishly tall, and so ... well, big. Fat, muscle, probably a lot of both. Dad would say she was hefty. She wasn't young, but wasn't old either; so, maybe that's what it means to be in your thirties or forties. She looked like she didn't take bad news well. She'd probably make a good jail guard.

"Welcome to Camp JCC," Mrs. Meyers said. "If everyone coming in could please go over to that side table and get a name tag before taking a seat. We'll get started in just a minute."

I did as she instructed, covertly looking from side to side, checking out names people were writing down.

"I see some familiar faces and some new faces," Mrs. Meyers said to no one in particular. "I'm looking forward to another terrific summer. We have some great things in store for our campers."

Once all the counselors were seated, Mrs. Meyers spent about a half-hour reading from a rulebook. She covered the daily activity flow and rules for counselors like attendance and proper behavior. If we were late more than three times, we were booted from camp. Forever. There was a dress code and safety guidelines. Then, there was the talk about lockdown drills we'd need to have later in the day, along with the CPR class.

After the monotonous rules rundown, Mrs. Meyers said it was time for an activity to get to know one another.

"Go ahead and pair up," she instructed. "We're going to do an icebreaker." I found this particularly funny since she was the one who seemed like a chunk of ice in need of breaking. "You're each going to ask your partner a list of questions, like an interview. After you're done, we'll come back together and you'll introduce your partner to the group."

"When you're finished," Mrs. Meyers called over the chatter, "turn back and face forward so I know you're done."

Like everyone else, I turned to the person next to me. She wasn't someone I'd ever seen around the JCC before. She was tough looking and wore her hair in a pixie cut with a few straw-like strands that fought to hide her cool, sharp, grey eyes. I'm guessing that she'd never set foot in a hair salon. That cut could only come from a pair of kitchen scissors. Her body language screamed "I don't want to be here!" as she sat with her arms crossed and her hands dug into her armpits. There wasn't an ounce of fat on her and her muscles were all perfectly toned. I was pretty fit, but there were certainly soft spots, as Aunt Deborah pointed out last time we were at her neighborhood pool. I looked around the room at all the other more normal-looking girls and wondered how I ended up with such bad luck.

"Okay," I began, mustering a bit of chipper to overcome the wolf. The list seemed easy enough. "First question: What's your name?"

"Alexa Striker," she said, looking down at the floor, then out the window, anywhere but at me. "But you should call me Lex. Everyone does."

I couldn't tell from the way she said it if she was happy or frustrated that people called her by this nickname. "Alexa" was so powerful and beautiful, but then again, I was never going to let anyone call me Katrina, so yeah, I got it. "Okay, Lex," I hesitated, repeating it back as I wrote it down on the ice-breaker form.

"What's the next question?" she snapped.

"Uh, let me see."

She was long and lanky but strong in the shoulders. I guessed by her build that gymnastics was her sport, a question I spotted on the list a few questions down.

"Okay, what town do you live in?"

"Margate."

"Me, too!"

Lex rolled her eyes. The camp was in Margate. I supposed that just about everyone in the room probably lived in Margate. Geez, she made me uncomfortable.

"How many more questions?" she sighed, staring at the clock on the gym wall.

"Just a few. What grade are you in? What's your area of specialty at camp? And what's one interesting thing about you?"

"I'm going to be a sophomore, I specialize in gymnastics, and I'm color blind."

74

"Color blind? I've never met anyone whose color blind. So that's real? Can you tell the difference between blue and ... ."

She cut me off. "Your turn." Lex yanked the list of questions and pen out of my hand. I tried to impress her by remembering all the questions before she could ask but then wondered why I felt the need to impress her.

"My name is Kit Carlin. I live in Margate. I guess I already told you that. I'll be a sophomore next year. I also specialize in gymnastics and I'd guessed that you did too, because you kinda look like a gymnast." I looked up for connection and got another eye roll. "Something interesting ... let me think ...," I knew I had to come up with something good. "I can tread water for thirty minutes."

"Oh yeah?" She shot me a look of disbelief.

"I had to do it one time for Girl Scouts. I was the only one in my troop left in the water after the thirty-minute bell rang." She looked like she still didn't believe me. "No joke."

"Okay, everyone," Mrs. Meyers called. We took turns around the circle introducing our partners to the rest of the group. Aside from Lex and myself, there was a girl named Sherry who seemed quite full of herself without having any apparent reason to be. She had a horrible case of acne and unmanageable, kinky, red hair. Sherry was a bit on the pudgy side and tried to hide it by wearing a T-shirt that was too large.

There were two Lisas: one was into swimming, the other, tennis. One of the Lisas was, for sure, a Shoobee from Philly. Many of the counselors and kids were Shoobees; they really lived in Philadelphia or New York, but they owned second homes at the shore and came down for the summer. Once Labor Day came, they were out of here.

Dad said when he was in junior high, he and his friends would go to the war memorial roundabout and wave goodbye as the stream of cars headed out on the Atlantic City Expressway, Philadelphia-bound for the winter.

The other Lisa went to ACHS and was a year ahead of me. I'd seen her around and knew who she was, but we didn't have any friends in common. There were two guys, Zach and Michael, and by the end of the day I still couldn't tell who was who. There was also a very nerdy guy named Ted who I recognized from school. Apparently, he was spearheading chess and various other dork activities. There was another girl named Sabrina. Or was it Celeste? Whatever her name was, she was going to be Ted's female counterpart in the dork arena. The rest of us watched as the two of them made goo-goo eyes at each other. I guess it's true what they say: there's someone for everyone.

And then there was Jake. I had not been able to stop staring at Jake since I entered the JCC that morning. Jake was sculpted from the heavens, the embodiment of a Greek god. He had lusciously thick brown hair that I imagined combing my fingers through. His eyes were a soft, warm brown and vanished into slits when he smiled. He specialized in gymnastics. Could it be true? How many classes would we have together? I imagined him spotting me on the bars, reaching out his arms for me to fall into.

After the icebreakers were over, we toured the camp. I'd been going to the JCC since I could walk so I could easily have given the tour. Mrs. Meyers showed us the boys and girls locker rooms, and Lex and I watched in annoyance as the two Lisas argued with Sherry over which locker they got. Seriously? Who cares? Lex and I opted for the two on the end, away from the drama.

Our tour ended in the orientation room, and Mrs. Meyers passed out our schedules. I had gymnastics on Tuesday and Thursday afternoons, but the rest of my schedule was a disheartening mix of playground watch, lunch watch, and a rotating duty shift with the WeeBee campers, and then a naptime watch that seemed horridly boring.

Tyler and I had spent six of the last eight summers here, so nothing in the activity schedule should have surprised me. Now, I had to get used to being here without him. Everything brought back memories. When I passed the pool, I thought back to our first swimming lessons. Were we even four years old? When I passed the gym, I remembered the annual Purim celebration, the Jewish holiday that celebrates the Jews not getting slaughtered by someone bad. We'd gone with Ari that year. I'd dressed up as Queen Esther and then walked into a room full of Queen Esthers. I started to cry when I realized I was not unique. Tyler and I had our first hamantaschen that day, and it became our inside joke. Whenever anyone mentioned a bakery, we always said we'd only go if we could get hamantaschen. I guess it was funny because they were supposed to be this sweet dessert, but they were actually pretty gross. The fruit inside was usually apricot or prune or something else awful. A tear rolled down my face. No one would laugh at hamantaschens with me ever again.

Back in the gym, they served us subs for lunch. I hung out with the Lisas and Sherry, and was still weirded out by Lex's vibe. She sat in her seat and spent the whole time on her phone. I was half in and out of the conversation with the girls, but kept one ear tuned in the direction of Jake. He was with Zach and Mike talking sports and video games.

After lunch, I excused myself to go to the bathroom before the next meeting started. The walls had an empty echo of Tyler. When I got into the bathroom stall, I closed my eyes and could almost hear his voice screaming across the building. I left my eyes closed for a minute, trying to melt away. It was good to be here, out of the house for a change, but being "on" around all of these people all day was its own level of exhaustion.

Back in the gym, Mrs. Meyers left us alone to watch a boring video on the history of the camp. Ted, the dork, fell asleep and started snoring. Zach and Mike used their straws from lunch and interview paper to shoot spitballs into Ted's mouth. We were all in hysterics and Ted was still sleeping, but Mrs. Meyers came back in to see what all the noise was about. No one was caught, but none of us could stop laughing. Mrs. Meyers had to wake Ted up when the video was over.

Our CPR and first-aid lessons were next. As I bent over to place my lips on the plastic dummy, I thought about placing my lips on Jake instead. When I looked up from the dummy, Jake was right across from me. We made eye contact and shared a "Isn't this dumb?" smile. It would be two days before I'd see that smile again. It was going to be a long weekend.

* * * *

When I got home, I thumbed through the mail. Even though it was always just bills, junk, and catalogs, I never stopped hoping there would be something special for me. At the bottom of the pile, a postcard slipped down to the floor. I dropped the rest of the mail on the kitchen table and picked it up. The front was a beach scene with surfers and "California" was splayed across the entire card in neon blue.

I flipped it over and read Brandon's note.

Kit,
Having an awesome time in Cali! So far we've gone to a wild animal park and SeaWorld. Tomorrow we go to Mexico for the day – muy bueno! I can practice my Spanish for real instead of in a stupid class. I so wish you were here. It's fun but it would be even better if one of my friends were here to share it.
Back next week!   Brandon

I re-read "I so wish you were here" over and over, wondering if he meant that he wished I was there or that any friend would do. I took the card up to my room and tacked it to my corkboard, text side out.

The first day of actual camp was hell. The kids were exhausting, and they never stopped screaming, and running, and crying, and scraping knees, and stubbing toes. I don't remember Tyler and I being quite so hysterical. Maybe we were.

By lunchtime, I had already taken care of a bee sting and bandaged a nasty cut. I guess that first-aid lesson was more important than I'd realized. The entire walk home, all I could think about was lying on the chaise on our deck and falling asleep in the sun.

A few years back, Dad had bought an old jukebox and had rigged it up so that the speakers faced the yard. Mom and Dad loaded it with their massive collection of 45s from the sixties, seventies, and eighties. You could queue up ten songs at a time, and then listen to them on the deck. The jukebox was one of Dad's best ideas. I decided today was a sixties kind of day. The lineup would definitely include *Norwegian Wood* by The Beatles, though, in all honesty, I always included that one no matter the decade. *I Put a Spell on You* — the Creedence Clearwater Revival version, the Rolling Stones' (I Can't Get No) Satisfaction, *and Hello, I Love You* by The Doors. That last one was in honor of Jake.

When I got home, Mom told me that Cousin Linda needed to change her plans so she was coming over for dinner tonight instead of tomorrow. I saw Mom's first smile in weeks this past weekend when Linda called to say that she would take "the case" and help us sue the guy who hit Tyler. So the afternoon turned into helping Mom clean up the house. So much for lounging in the sun.

Linda wasn't planning on being there until seven, which upset Mom. She had to eat no later than six or she would complain about indigestion all night long. Mom was busy putting the final touches on the famous lasagna that she always saved for guests. She practically stole the recipe from our old neighbors, the Carlettos, before they moved back to Philly.

"Mom, I vacuumed all of downstairs and cleaned the guest bathroom. Is there anything else you need me to do?"

"Could you set the table?"

"Sure. Is Dad coming home for dinner?" This was now a nightly question.

"He's at the marina working on Dr. Cohen's boat," Mom said, but in a way that suggested that's where she hoped he would be, or, I feared, in a way that said she didn't really care where he was or if he came home at all. It seemed more likely to me that he was at the bar at the marina drinking with Dr. Cohen.

"Should I set a place for him?" That was really my question.

"Umm ... go ahead." Her answer meant that I'd be returning the same table setting back to the cabinet after dinner, clean and unused. "After the table's set, why don't you go up and change for dinner. Put something nice on, maybe that beige sundress Grandma bought you. We're going to have a nice dinner." Mom sounded sure. It was comforting to have her in control again, even if it was just about dinner.

Linda arrived promptly, like she always did. I wondered if that was a trait all lawyers shared. My old friend Ashley's dad is a lawyer, and she would get in so much trouble if she was even five minutes late. Weird, I never heard from her family after Tyler died. Surely they knew. Well, maybe they didn't. Maybe there were a ton of people who had no clue. It's not like everyone reads the obituaries. But all the moms are on Facebook together, so there's that.

"So tell me how your summer's going, sweetie," Linda asked as we started our salads. Dad wasn't home yet.

"Oh, it's okay. I'm working at the JCC."

"You're a camp counselor, right?"

"Counselor-in-training. Not to be confused with camp counselor. I'm specializing in gymnastics, of course."

Linda nodded. She'd attended many of my gymnastic meets over the years.

"How old are the children you work with?" She was barely picking at her salad. Linda never ate much. I couldn't imagine how she wasn't hungry all the time. Mom says I eat like a horse, but any time I try and picture that it totally grosses me out.

"I have different age groups each day, but mostly they're anywhere from six to twelve. If you're under six, you have to go to the daycare, and if you're over twelve, well, you shouldn't be there."

"So will you be a regular counselor next year?"

"I think so. Sometimes they may make you be a CIT for more than one year. I'm not sure how that works."

"Ah, makes sense that you would need to be a CIT first. So, any special boy in your life?"

The dreaded boyfriend question. Why do adults think it's any of their business? Wouldn't the whole world know if I had a boyfriend?

"Kit doesn't date," Mom answered for me.

"Excuse me?" I nearly coughed out the words. Did she really just say that? I don't date? Like I don't want to? What the hell?

"Well, you're not really into boys."

"Well, I'm not into girls." Seriously, we weren't having this conversation.

"I didn't say that. It was Tyler who had the love bug," she said. "He was the one always with a girlfriend. Kit just hasn't quite gotten there yet."

This was insane. Mom honestly thought I didn't date by choice? I hadn't "gotten there yet"? What the hell? I'd been tongue-tied and stumbly over Jake for the past twelve hours!

"Oh, yes, Tyler was quite the love bug, wasn't he!" Linda squealed.

"I'm done." I pushed my chair away and made it scrape across the wood floor as loudly as I could. Mom and Linda gave me that stupid adult face that said they really had no idea why I would be upset. I took my plate into the kitchen.

Dad strolled in the front door well after dinner. From my room, I could hear their conversation.

"Where's dinner?" Dad demanded.

"There's lasagna in the fridge. Heat it up."

"You're done already?"

"Dinner was at seven, Jeff. It's now eight-thirty. You do the math."

Oh, that was going to trigger a fight. So I slammed my door and blasted my music as Dad kept yelling. Whatever.

A half-hour later, things were eerily quiet, but Linda's car was still in the driveway. I cracked my door so I could hear what they were talking about.

"So what you're saying, then," Mom was saying in a very businesslike and serious tone, "is that since Tyler wasn't wearing reflectors, we don't have a case?"

"Yes, Susan. This is what she's been trying to get across to you for weeks. If there was a court case here, Linda would tell us," Dad said.

"I'm only trying to keep you from being disappointed. Our best bet would be to settle this out of court."

"Oh no! This man is going to stand trial for what he did!" Mom's voice was quaking. My heart hurt for her and I ran downstairs to check on things.

Dad pulled out a chair for me and tapped it, indicating I should sit down. I assumed the gesture was to show Linda how our family was still normal.

"Moneywise, I'm not sure what we can get. Maybe fifty-thousand, max."

"Oh, come on, this has to be worth at least a half a mil." Mom was negotiating the way Dad did at a boat auction.

It was disgusting and I had to say something. "What do we need this guy's money for? How do you turn Tyler's life into a dollar amount?"

"Kit, wake up! This man has put such a level of stress upon my life that it's amazing I haven't been committed!"

"We can't bring Tyler back! I don't know about you, but that's all I want! Not some stranger's money!" I cried, barely holding back my tears.

To my complete shock, Dad reached over and squeezed my knee. It was the first gesture of kindness Dad had made since, well, since that night we sat in the ER waiting to hear from the doctor. Dad had his arm around me that night, but as soon as the doctor pronounced Tyler dead, Dad let go. He hadn't reached out since.

Mom ignored me, and she and Linda kept talking about the case. When Dad excused himself to go to the garage, I went upstairs and straight into Tyler's room.

I tried to wrap my head around why Mom was so eager to hurt the guy who hit Tyler. The way I figured it, he'd already suffered enough. He woke up every day and was forced to remember what he'd done. Regardless, Mom wanted justice. No, she wanted revenge. In her mind, nothing would be right until she saw this guy suffer horribly. Maybe that's the difference between Mom and Dad. When all the layers were stripped away, it came down to the Jewish God who preached "an eye for an eye" versus the Christian God of "turn the other cheek." My parents didn't practice a religion, but was it hard coded in their DNA? And if it was, where did that leave me?

I pulled out the lyric book and flipped it open to an empty page.

June 27

Tyler,

Well, Mom and Cousin Linda are downstairs plotting how they're going to kill the man who hit you. I feel like showing them your button, "Why do we kill people who kill people to show people that killing people is wrong?" Wouldn't that piss them off? I seriously think Mom wants this guy to get the death penalty for hitting you. Oddly, Dad and I are on the same page on this one.

Can you believe I just finished my first day of work and neither Mom nor Dad asked me how my day was? I'll tell you, though. It was okay. Things are sort of a mess because they're still working out scheduling problems. There was a lot of confusion, but I've got some sweet kids in my classes. I'm looking forward to teaching gymnastics. I've been practicing in the basement every night.

It sucks being alive without you. Last night, I couldn't stop shaking in bed and it wasn't even cold outside. I put on this fakey, pretend personality when I go to camp so I can make it through the day without crying. Last week, Mom told me that I didn't have to take the job if I didn't want to. I think the only thing worse than having to *get through camp would be spending days alone at home.*

I'm going to make it though, don't you worry about me. I'm still "Kit the Kid," tough as nails.

All my love,

K

I buried my nose deep in his pillow. It still smelled like him.

Chapter Nine

"You're late," Lex called, hands on her hips and forehead furrowed.

"Sorry," I said, eyeing the clock in the gymnasium. It was three minutes past the hour.

"I hate it when people are late. Don't be late again."

"I didn't know you were in charge," I spat back.

"You wanna start something?" she threatened, taking a step toward me. I'd never been in a fight, not a real fight anyway, with punching and stuff. I wasn't about to get into one here with her in the middle of the JCC. The campers were watching us with their mouths wide open and bugged-out eyes.

"Let's start teaching, huh, Lex?" I looked toward the kids. Something in my tone must have jolted her out of whatever weird space she was in and we began class. By the end of it, the soft-spoken kids had gravitated toward me and the louder kids hovered around Lex like a swarm of flies.

"Bye," I called as I dashed out of the room.

"Wait a sec." Lex grabbed her things and caught up with me. So much for my quick escape.

"How long have you been doing gymnastics?" she asked in a rather snotty tone.

"Long enough," I said, picking up my pace so she'd get the hint and drop back.

"You're good. I still can't do aerials as well as you." Her honesty caught me off guard and I slowed my pace.

"Thanks. I can't do half the stuff you did on the beam. I guess I need more room to move around. I've always been better at the floor."

"That was easy. We just figured out who'll be teaching what. Now we just have to settle on the bars and horse."

"Yeah," I smiled nervously. "Well, I've got playground duty. I can't be late," I said, putting emphasis on the last part. I got zero response out of her though, as if she didn't remember yelling at me an hour before.

✳ ✳ ✳ ✳

On my way to the locker room at the end of the day, I passed Jake. My heart fluttered at the sight of him, his confident shoulders and perfectly toned body. I looked toward the group he was with but singled him out, making eye contact as we passed. He smiled wide and winked as he walked by. I felt my face flush red, wondering what the wink meant. Did he do that to everyone? Inside the locker room, I was stuffing my dirty clothes into my backpack when someone tapped me on the shoulder.

"Hey."

"Oh, hi there." I turned around to see Lex. She had already changed out of her camp uniform and was wearing frayed cut-offs with a raunchy T-shirt that read Tiny's Texas Town with a picture of a man riding a woman like a bull. Guessing that one violated the no-logo T-shirts rule in the dress code.

"Wanna hit Galino's?"

"Sure," I said, without really thinking. Who doesn't say yes to ice cream? But ugh, with her? What was her deal? I guess my curiosity wanted to know.

We walked down Jerome Avenue. Lex seemed like she was from somewhere else. Even her walk was confident and intense, like she lived in a city. I couldn't picture her as a Shoobee, though. "So, did you grow up in Margate?" I asked to break the uncomfortable silence.

"New York. Brooklyn, actually, but I'll be living here now with my aunt. You could say I'm sort of in between homes."

Shoobees didn't come from places like Brooklyn. "Do you like it here?"

"Eh." She shrugged her shoulders. "It's pretty quiet. I miss the city."

"Where are your parents?" As soon as the question left my mouth, I realized I shouldn't have asked. Lex turned blank the way I do when people ask about Tyler. I knew what her answer was before she could say it. She turned her gaze away from me.

"I'm so sorry." I knew just saying it wasn't going to help. "I didn't know ..."

"Don't be sorry," she said, cutting me off.

I desperately wanted to run home and hug Mom. I couldn't imagine. Both parents. Geez.

"The Lisas told me you lost your brother this summer. We have more in common than we think."

I tried hard to imagine having anything in common with Lex. She probably smoked cigarettes and shoplifted and did a bazillion things on a regular basis that I would never dream of doing in a million years.

"Do you have any other brothers or sisters?"

"Nope." I shook my head, still rather dazed. "Now it's just me and my mouse, Morrison."

"You have a mouse?"

"Yeah, it was Tyler's." Was. That damn word. I pushed back the tears. I did not need to fall apart in front of Lex.

"I want to get a snake but my aunt won't let me."

"Snakes are cool," I said as we turned the corner and walked toward Galino's. "Just don't let your future snake near my mouse!"

Lex smiled and I saw a twinkle in her eye and laugh-line wrinkles around her eye suggesting that she had, in fact, smiled and laughed before.

"How about you? Do you have any brothers or sisters?"

"I have one older brother, Rick. He's in the Naval Academy at Annapolis. He said I could visit him this summer. I can't wait," Lex said as we approached the counter at Galino's. "What's your vice?"

"My what?"

"What do you like to get?" Lex giggled, making me feel stupid.

"I usually get a chocolate soft serve with jimmies."

"Jimmies?"

"You know, sprinkles."

"Ah, yeah. That's what I get, too."

I eyed her suspiciously. Of all the people to have things in common with, why did it have to be her? I should be here with the Lisas … or Jake.

We ordered our cones and found an empty table in the back. Galino's was a big hangout for all of the counselors and kids at the JCC, so finding an empty table was a major achievement.

"Which high school are you going to go to?" It was a challenge to lick all the dripping ice cream before it reached my hand and maintain a conversation at the same time. I'd always thought that there should be an unspoken rule that you don't talk until your ice cream is under control.

"So far it's still Holy Spirit."

"Holy Spirit? Aren't you Jewish?"

"Nope!"

"If you're Catholic, what are you doing working at the JCC?"

"You don't have to be Jewish to work there. Besides, I have a lot of experience teaching gymnastics. There aren't any Catholic camps on this island and I don't have a car, so here I am. Praise Allah!" Lex shrugged her shoulders and sighed. She had so many freckles on her arms that I couldn't tell where they ended. They all sort of merged together like a lace shawl that covered every part of her.

"Allah is Muslim," I laughed.

"I know," Lex smiled mischievously. This girl was strange.

"So what do you mean by it's still Holy Spirit?"

"I'm not a good Catholic girl, and I'm best off going to a public high school. No sense spending the extra money, the public school system's good enough for me. Now I'm working hard to convince my aunt of that fact. If she had the money, I'd be at a fancy boarding school in New York."

Lex pushed away the strands of hair that always hung in her face, and sucked at the bottom of her cone, making a loud slurping sound. She sounded exactly like Tyler when he did that.

"My old friends go to Holy Spirit."

"Old?"

"Yeah, they stopped talking to me after they made the switch. They have their own group or clique now. Whatever."

"Sound like anti-friends, not old friends. The island isn't that big. You still run into each other, right?"

I shrugged my shoulders in reply and changed the subject. "So I don't understand how you can be a full counselor and not a counselor-in-training if you're only a sophomore."

"I turn sixteen in September. Let's put it this way: I've already been a sophomore."

I didn't know any girls who'd ever been held back. I could think of a couple of guys but they had been real screw-offs. I wondered how bad your grades had to be to have been held back. Was she dumb or did she just not care? Or maybe it all had to do with when and how her parents died. What would my freshman year have looked like if Tyler died in the middle? "I turned fifteen in May," was all I could think to say.

"What do you do for fun?"

I was grateful she changed the subject.

"I mostly hang out with my bro ... ." I started to say "my brother and Brandon." "I mean my brother's friend, Brandon. We go to the beach, swim at his pool ..."

"Friend or boyfriend?" Lex asked, her eyebrows raised.

"Friend. He was my brother's best friend."

"Gotcha. Well, this has been fun. I need to head home and help my aunt with some stuff. See you tomorrow."

I was only halfway through my cone and I thought we were in the midst of a conversation. Was she really ditching me? Very strange. But then again, there wasn't much about Lex that was very normal.

I left when Lex did and walked the rest of the way home. As I fumbled for my house keys to open the front door, my phone started ringing from deep in my backpack. I tried to find it before the call went to voicemail.

"Kitarino!" Brandon called into the phone with a thick surfer drawl.

"Brandon! Are you back?"

"Yeah, I got back really late last night. I'm all messed up with the time-zone difference. My Aunt Janet in Philly got me at the airport and I spent the night at her place. Then my Mom came and got me this morning. I'm totally exhausted. I spent the whole day in the pool."

"You bum! I worked my butt off today. I can't wait to hear about your trip."

"Did you get my postcard?"

"Yeah, it came on Friday," I said, thinking of how I re-read it over and over throughout the weekend.

"Mexico was killer. When we drove back, we had to wait in line for like two hours to get back into the U.S. Kids were selling Disney crap like towels from movies that were popular four years ago and these bizarro ceramic pigs. It was crazy."

"Wow."

"Yeah, Tijuana is only a half-hour from San Diego. Listen, are you doing anything tonight?"

"No, and I'm dying for a night out of this house."

"Cool. See if you can come over. My parents are going out and I have to babysit Jason. Don't eat dinner 'cause they're going to order pizza before they leave."

"Let me check with my mom and I'll call you right back."

"Okay." He hung up.

I went to find Mom, but her car wasn't in the driveway. No note and no explanation. This was getting old. She only worked three days a week at the clinic, and today was one of her days off. Where was she? I decided to take off without leaving a note. If she didn't have to, why should I? Maybe that would teach her a lesson.

"Oh, hey! I thought you were going to call me back!" he said as he opened the door and grabbed me in his arms. His hug was so tight and so strong and so completely comforting.

"My mom left again without saying anything to me so ... Oh my God! You cut off all your hair!"

"What do you think?"

"I don't know ..."

"You hate it, don't you?" Brandon's sensitive side always cracked me up.

"No, actually, it looks pretty cool. Your eyes really pop out now. Wow! I'll have to get used to it." I laughed, ruffling his short, spiky hair.

"One of my uncle's neighbors is a professional surfer and he had a cut like this. I thought it looked cool."

I thought back to how Crissy loved Brandon's longish hair and wondered why I knew so many details of their relationship. She'd be freaked.

"It looks great, don't worry." I plopped down on his couch and let out a sigh. "I'm so glad you're back. My parents are driving me nuts! I have to call when I'm going to be late. I have to ask permission to leave. But they come and go as they please and don't tell me a thing."

"Hi, Kit! Hi, Kit! Hi, Kit!" Brandon's brother Jason came running into the living room followed by his ever-present sidekick, Daniel, a mousy little boy with curly brown hair and the complete opposite of Jason.

"Hi, Jason! How's it going?" I scooped him into my arms and twirled him around the room, our usual move. "Hi, Daniel," I whispered and he blushed, yelped, and raced back downstairs. Brandon had one of those cool upside down split-level houses where the den and kids' rooms were on the first floor and the formal living room, dining room, kitchen and parent's room were on the second. The front door was on the landing between the floors.

"Jason, you cut your hair, too! Now you look just like your brother."

"Monkey see, monkey do," Brandon smiled at Jason. "He made me take him to the barber today."

"So how was first grade?"

"Stinky! I didn't like my teacher."

I tried to ruffle his spiky hair but it was crunchy with gel. "Your brother and I both had Mrs. McDuffery ..." – I dropped my voice to a whisper – "and we didn't like her either."

Jason laughed. "Um, um, um, Kit? Do you want to come down and play video games with me and Daniel?"

"No, I think I'll hang out up here with your brother."

"Please, please, please ...," he begged.

"Maybe next time."

"You promise?"

"We'll see," I smiled at Brandon.

"Okay, then, twirl me again if you won't promise."

I twirled Jason right onto the stairs leading down to the playroom. "Does that Daniel kid live here?" I asked Brandon.

"It seems that way, doesn't it?"

"So, what are your parents doing tonight?" I asked as we walked into the living room and sat down on the couches.

"They're going out to dinner with some friends and then they're all seeing Barry Manilow at Resorts." Brandon made a gagging noise.

"Ewww. Isn't he that cheesy '70s singer?" I stuck out my tongue.

Brandon nodded.

"I'm so hungry. I've barely eaten all day. What kind of pizza did you order?"

"Pepperoni. D'Napoli's, of course."

I gave him the thumbs up sign.

Brandon turned on the TV with the remote.

"Survivor?" he asked.

I hesitated. Could we keep watching it? Should we? Tyler, Brandon, and I had been watching re-runs of the old show on Netflix every week after school. Was it okay to keep going without Tyler? Did I even want to? He'd never find out who survived. Guess he didn't survive. The thought popped out of some deep, dark, black humor place in my brain. What was wrong with me?

"Let's watch something else." As though Brandon was already thinking the same thing, he pulled up a show I'd never heard of, something with an airplane crash and a deserted island and enough of the same features as Survivor without being the same show that it worked. I gave him an approving nod and we settled into the couch, waiting for the pizza to arrive.

Ten minutes later, my phone rang. It was Mom. "Young lady, why aren't you home? And why is there no note?!" she screamed into the phone.

"There was no note from you when I got home!" I looked to Brandon for moral support, but he was playing with his phone and not paying attention. "You and Dad leave all the time without telling me where you're going. How come when I do the same, I get in trouble?"

"I don't want to hear you talking back to me. Now come home. It's time for dinner."

"Brandon's dad already ordered pizza. It would be rude for me to leave."

"All right, fine. I don't want to argue with you. Louise said you need your space."

I groaned. The doorbell rang and Brandon hopped up to get the door.

"What time will you be home?" Mom asked.

"What's my curfew?"

"You know your curfew."

"Then that's when I'll be home."

I hung up and screamed "ARGH!" at the top of my lungs. Brandon came running upstairs, nearly tripping and sending the pizza box flying across the living room floor.

"Are you okay?"

"Yeah, I'm fine," I said, dropping my head to my knees and shaking my hair toward the floor.

"Do you have to go home?"

"No."

Brandon called Daniel and Jason up for dinner. I got the bottle of cherry syrup from the fridge and poured enough to coat the bottom of each glass. Then I topped off the glasses with ice cubes, ginger ale and maraschino cherries.

"Okay, pizza and Shirley Temples are ready to go!" I sang as Jason and Daniel came running up the stairs.

Within ten minutes, there wasn't a trace of pizza left.

After dinner, we played with the kids until Daniel's mom picked him up and it was time to put Jason to bed. Brandon, Jason, and I piled into his bed and listened painfully as

Jason read us a book about the adventures of Fly Guy at the pace of a first grader, sounding out each long word.

Once Jason was asleep, we headed over to Brandon's room. It wasn't until I was there, alone with him in his room, that it hit me that we'd never hung out here without Tyler. It had always been the three of us at least, sometimes more with Crissy and Missy and others. We were like a tricycle that just grew up into a ten-speed overnight, but weren't ready to give up that extra wheel. I stopped myself before I spiraled into another bout of depression. Brandon was back. It was summer. We were still alive. It was time to live.

Brandon and I hung out in his room while he played DJ. The only classic rock he listened to was what Tyler was into: The Doors, a little bit of Rolling Stones, and Pink Floyd. Most of Brandon's music was modern stuff that Tyler and I hated. I thumbed through his stack of Rolling Stone magazines wishing he would play something I liked, but without Tyler there, it felt wrong to ask. I sighed when he played some DJ mash up and he shot me that look, about to give me the same old lecture about how I needed to broaden my horizons and join the century.

"Is your family still seeing that shrink?" he asked as he messed with his playlist on his phone.

"Yeah. My mom sees her twice a week, and my dad and I go with Mom once a week. I got to go by myself once and that was a little better. Going with my dad is horrible. I basically just sit there and don't say a word because whenever I talk, he makes rude grunts or comments." I loved lounging in Brandon's black vinyl beanbag. The coolness of the bag felt refreshing against my skin. It was barely the end of June, but the days were so miserably hot that it wasn't cooling down at all at night.

"That doesn't sound like your dad."

"Then you haven't met Post-Tyler Dad. He's changed."

"Uh-oh."

"Anyway, I don't want to talk about my dad," I said, sticking my nose back into the magazine.

"Okay. What do you all talk about with the shrink?"

"The stages of grief and what stage we're at." When I rolled my eyes, he giggled. "Mostly my mom breaks down and tells stories about Tyler as a kid. I feel so invisible. It's like I was a part of Tyler, and when he died they were surprised that I was still alive."

"That's creepy. I know your dad is excited to have me around this summer. He sent me three texts while I was gone. Did he not know that I was in Cali?"

"He did? That's weird. I don't know what my dad does or doesn't know. We don't talk much." I lifted my head up from the magazine to look at Brandon. "And don't say 'Cali.' You sound like a total dork!"

"Okay, Miss Queen of Cool," he smirked.

I blushed and stuck my face back in the magazine hoping he wouldn't notice.

"I guess he wants me to come by this weekend to help out at the shop. Said we can go sailing afterwards."

"That's nice," I snipped.

"You can come."

"Oh, I doubt that. Anyway, if my dad likes having you around, it's fine by me. You know, if I was at anyone else's house, I bet I would have had to go home. It's okay because I'm hanging out with you. I don't get it."

Brandon shook his head. "I guess it doesn't matter. Whatever makes them happy, ya know? I don't mind helping out. It's not like I have a job or anything."

"Don't rub it in," I threatened.

"So speaking of work, how is the new job going?" Brandon switched up the playlist to play a Beatles song. Finally something good!

"Fine. I made a new friend. Well, I think I did. She's pretty weird."

"Is she hot?"

"Brandon!" I threw the Rolling Stone at him. "As I was going to say, she's tough, like street tough. She's an orphan. Her parents must have died sometime recently because she just moved in with her aunt."

"Man! How did they die?"

"She didn't tell me. I didn't want to ask. I think it's a little weird that the one friend I've made this summer happens to have lost her parents. It makes me realize that it could be worse. I could have lost more than Tyler." My eyes slowly welled up with tears as I spoke, and the last part of the sentence barely squeaked out.

"And I'm not going anywhere," Brandon said, as if reading my mind. He walked over and offered his hand to help me out of the beanbag. The gesture seemed extra sweet, even for Brandon. "Did you bring your suit?"

"No," I mumbled through the tears. "I left the house too fast and I forgot." I quickly wiped the tears from my face, trying to pretend they never escaped.

"Do you think you can wear one of my mom's?"

"Uh, Brandon, your mom is about ten times as big as me," I said, laughing and crying at the same time. Brandon was smirking. "I can swim in my tank top and shorts."

"Are you sure?"

"Yeah, no problem. Can I borrow a T-shirt for later?"

"Of course. We could always go skinny dipping," Brandon suggested with a mischievous grin. Brandon was joking, of course, but the question brought a chill to me and I self-consciously crossed my arms over my chest. What exactly was happening here? Maybe he wasn't joking? Then what did that mean?

"Not with you," I answered flatly, playfully smacking him.

"Your loss," he laughed back.

The lights of the pool created an iridescent glow across the patio and I silently thanked God for allowing me another summer of late-night swims serenaded by crickets. I thanked God for leaving me Brandon.

I made it home before curfew and my parents were already asleep so they didn't notice me going into Tyler's room. I got out the journal and began writing.

June 29th

Dear Tyler—

I'm sorry I didn't write the last few nights. Can you even tell time where you are? Do you know what day of the week it is or do the days just merge into one? I guess if the sun doesn't rise and set, you might never know. I think that would be so cool, to not have time. Is it dark or cold where you are? I wish we could talk.

I just got back from hanging out with Brandon. We were laughing about that time the three of us were playing on the porch of his old house, when he used to live across the street from us. Remember the blizzard, when it took the garbage company a whole week to find snowplow attachments and dig out the city? The snow came up to the level of the porch, maybe five feet, and we dared each other to jump in.

You were the first one off the porch and then you got stuck. We were too scared to ask for help, so we let you sit there until you started crying. Then I went to our other neighbors' to get that

nanny they had living with them to dig you out.
Mom and Dad came outside right when the nanny
was reaching through the snow to rescue you. You
may not remember it as funny but we were bustin'
our guts laughing so hard. I guess you won't have
to deal with any more snowstorms!

I felt like such a phony writing about Brandon as if nothing were happening. But really, what the hell was happening? Was I allowed to like Brandon? It's not like Brandon was going to leave Crissy for me. The whole thing was wrong and ridiculous and besides, I had to focus my efforts on Jake. None of my messy love life was Tyler's concern. I'd never kept anything from Tyler, but this, well ...

Well, I'm pretty sleepy and I have camp
tomorrow. I'll write more soon.
    Love ya! K

Chapter Ten

I couldn't believe it was already the Fourth of July. Where had the summer gone? It had been six weeks since the accident. We all began calling it "the accident," which made it sound as if Tyler were merely hurt – perhaps in the hospital – and that he'd be back home soon.

"What should we do tonight?" I asked at breakfast as I sliced my blueberry pancakes into bite-sized pieces.

"I think there's a new episode of that reality chase show. Maybe we'll watch that," Mom said, her gaze drifting to the faraway place she sought so she wouldn't have to look at me.

"We're not even going to watch the fireworks?" No response. I don't think we've ever not watched the fireworks. "Mom!"

"Oh, is today the fourth of July?"

"Uh, yeah."

"I think your father is going to a barbeque."

"You're not going with?"

She shook her head no.

I wondered if I was invited, but decided that even if I was, I didn't want to be alone with Dad. He probably wouldn't want me to go unless I brought Brandon anyway, and Brandon was going to the big ACHS party. Brandon tried to get me to go, but I still wasn't ready to face everyone and their pity. Maybe I should just hang out with Lex.

After breakfast, Mom asked me to go to Weiss's to pick up some groceries.

"Are you going to ride your bike?" she asked, her voice full of fear.

"Mom, I ride it all the time. I'll be fine."

"It doesn't take that long to walk, you know." The pleading tone in her voice made me cringe.

"I'll be okay." I kissed her on the forehead like I was the mom and she was the kid.

As I rode through the neighborhood, I felt weird and out of place, like some kind of alien wondering why everything was blanketed in red, white, and blue. American flags were everywhere. I don't know why I expected the rest of the world to stop celebrating just because I felt like I never could again.

It wasn't until I entered Weiss's that I remembered what it meant to be in Margate on the Fourth of July. From the back of a long line, I watched the deli clerks scoop buckets of coleslaw out of huge plastic garbage cans. The line was at least thirty people long, and I was inching my way through the crowd to get to the dairy section when I heard someone call out my name.

"Kit? Kit Carlin! Well, how the heck are you?" It was our old neighbor, Mr. Carletto, with his wife. What were they doing here? They moved to Philly a few years ago when he got a new job.

"We're in town visiting Lorraine's folks for the weekend. How's your family? How's that crazy brother of yours?"

I stood frozen in place, my Keds stuck to the shiny linoleum floor. I didn't know how to say what I needed to say.

"Tyler's dead," I blurted out, realizing afterward that I sounded like Lex did when she told me about her parents. Their faces turned white and I wished I'd lied.

Then came an awkward silence, and I fidgeted as I waited for them to respond. I felt like the entire store had their eyes on me, but when I looked around no one was watching us.

"Oh my!" Mrs. Carletto gasped, putting her hand over her mouth. Mr. Carletto looked equally stunned. I didn't know what to do next.

"When?" she whispered from behind her hand.

"At the beginning of the summer. He was hit by a car on his bike." Why couldn't Mom get her own damn milk and eggs?

"This is terrible, just terrible." It was obvious Mrs. Carletto had no more clue what to say than I did.

"I've got to get some things for my mom. I'll see you later." I turned away without waiting for a reply.

"Wait, do you need a ride home? Let us drop you off," Mrs. Carletto called after me.

"No thank you," I said.

"Okay. Well, please give our love to your family."

"I will," I said, and burst into tears the second I was out of their sight.

I didn't tell Mom about the Carlettos and maybe that was a bad decision, but whatever. After the Carletto run-in, I was certain there was no way I wanted to be at that ACHS party. I wanted to hide under the covers.

I dropped the groceries off at home and then got back on my bike and disappeared for the afternoon. I rode in circles around neighborhoods. I just kept riding.

When I got home, hours later, Dad had already left for whatever barbeque he was going to and Mom was glued to the couch, watching TV. It seemed the only time she ever came to life anymore was if the discussion involved the trial.

"Brandon called for you," Mom said without looking away from the TV. I wondered why he didn't call my phone, but when I looked down I saw a bunch of missed texts. I'd never even thought to check it today.

"Was it about the party?"

"He didn't say."

"Well, I'm not going."

"Stay home with me. We can be lazy, eat frozen pizzas, and make popcorn."

That sounded really good. But the fireworks. Who doesn't watch the fireworks on the 4th? What kind of weirdo, zombie family were we becoming?

"Okay." I plopped down on the couch, pushing Mom's feet out of the way.

We watched Wheel of Fortune while we ate our pizza from TV trays. After that, we clicked over to PBS's Fourth of July special, but it was just a bunch of boring symphony music that was putting me to sleep. I told Mom that I was going to read, but on my way to my room, I looked up and saw the trap door leading to the attic.

It had been ages since I'd been up there. When Tyler and I were really little and couldn't handle fireworks noise up close, Dad would take us to the attic to watch the fireworks over the water in Atlantic City through the attic window.

Carefully, I tugged on the cord that released the ladder, but the trap door flew open and the ladder knocked me in the head as it came crashing down. I fell in a heap on the floor and held my throbbing head. My hand shook its way toward my face and I was horrified to see my fingernails covered with blood.

"Mom!" I cried, but she must have heard the crash because she was already beside me before I finished screaming.

"What happened?" Mom took me in her arms and I started sobbing like I was five and I'd scraped my knee. I couldn't remember the last time she held me in her arms and I wished that I could just be little again. "Let me see," she said, gently parting my hair.

"Ow!"

"Honey, I have to see," she cooed like a good mom and my instincts pulled me right back to her, letting her secure my head in her cradled hands. "It doesn't look that bad, actually. There's a little blood, but the cut isn't deep. You'll be fine. Let me get something to clean it up."

Mom returned with a soft pink lukewarm washcloth, which felt both painful and soothing at the same time. She laid it against my scalp and wiped away the blood.

"All better," Mom said, tapping me on the shoulder and taking the washcloth back to the bathroom.

"Thanks. Do you want to come up and watch the fireworks with me?"

She shook her head and walked back downstairs into zombieland.

I used the ladder to steady myself and although I was a bit dizzy, I climbed up fine. The attic was dustier than I remembered and smelled of mothballs and dampness. Everything was blanketed in memories.

Sitting on Mom's hope chest, I looked around at the boxed-up history of my family's life. In the corner was the rocking horse that Tyler and I always fought to ride, — its red velvet worn off the saddle. Mom's knitting supplies spilled over a basket grey with dust. Half a baby blanket lay on top — her last project, unfinished. The boxes marked "Tyler" seemed lost up here amongst all of our things, as if they were merely waiting for a new delivery address.

I was off in la la land, wondering if we were ever going to pack up Tyler's room, when I heard a creak on the attic stairs. "Mom, is that you?" I called with a bit of shakiness in my voice. I wanted to be brave about hanging out in the attic, but it was an attic after all, and it took a fair bit of courage to be up there alone at night.

"No, it's me," Brandon's voice called back.

"Brandon! What are you doing here?" I ran to the top of the stairs.

"I just left the party. I figured you'd be here."

"You bugged me so much to go!"

"Yeah, but you didn't."

"So?"

"I don't know. I wasn't in a party mood."

Brandon was always in a party mood. He walked to the window, rested his elbows on the sill, and perched his chin on his hands.

"Did Tyler ever bring you up here?" I asked, joining him at the window.

He shook his head no just as the sky exploded in color. The view faced directly toward Atlantic City where the show always shot out over the beach, the colors reflecting on the ocean.

"Do I smell beer?" I said.

"Maybe."

"Brandon!"

"Oh, don't 'Brandon' me, Kit. You should loosen up a bit."

"I'm loose," I said jamming my fists into my hips and thrusting them to the left.

"Oh, right," he laughed and then started tickling me like crazy. We both fell to the floor laughing while the next explosion of red, white, and blue opened up in the shape of the American flag beyond the window.

"How do you think you get a job designing firework shows?" Brandon asked, helping me up off the floor.

"I have no idea. Maybe there's a school you have to go to." I shrugged my shoulders. Brandon always came up with the most bizarre questions.

"That would be the coolest job. I'll have to remember that one."

"So, who was at the party?"

"It was mostly the Longport crowd you can't stand — Melissa and the other cheerleaders — but there were also some guys from track, the usual suspects. Dylan Ryerson asked a lot about you."

"Really? You know, now that you mention it, he sent a really huge bouquet of roses after the funeral."

"Someone has a crush on Kit," Brandon taunted.

"Whatever. I barely even know the guy," I fired back, fake-punching him in the arm.

Brandon placed his arms behind him and leaned back, snickering.

"Stop it!" I whined. "I can't believe you'd rather be cramped in this hot attic watching fireworks out of a window than partying with everyone."

"Yeah, well, it didn't feel right there without Tyler. It's just not right. I'm not handling this much better than you. You know that, don't you? He pretty much screwed us both up."

"So how are we supposed to get through this?" Suddenly, I started crying and felt like a fool. It seemed I was always crying in front of Brandon. Honestly, how could he still like hanging out with me? I must remind him of Tyler and that had to get old eventually.

Brandon leaned closer and put his arms around me to comfort me, but there was something more to it, and I let my face fall on his shoulder. He rubbed my back and whispered, "It's okay. It's going to be okay," and he squeezed harder and harder, like maybe he could squeeze the ache right out of me.

When I finally started to move away, he held on tight to my arms, then cupped a hand around my face and wiped away a few of my tears. He was crying too, and I reached up to wipe away his tears, but he grabbed my hand and pushed it gently toward his lips, and with the softest of touches, his lips kissed my palm. My heart raced so fast that I was sure it would speed up and leap right out of my mouth. I tried Grandma's deep-breathing technique, but that only made it worse. It wasn't the tender comfort of a brother, but something more. I didn't know if it was the alcohol or if maybe there was always supposed to be something more between Brandon and me.

Brandon's eyes locked on mine as he pulled my head closer to his. Our lips touched. I wished I'd put on my cherry lip-gloss and that the taste of Brandon's mouth was something like pizza instead of beer, but otherwise it was perfect. Our lips melded together and his tongue gently glided into my mouth, searching for mine, for me, for connection. I pressed harder into his hold, our mouths locked so that not even air could get in. Brandon wrapped his arms around me and I wanted to disappear into him. As his hand reached up my shirt, the loudest firework of the show boomed across the room, causing us both to fall backward as if it had come right through the attic window and pushed us to the floor. I gazed at Brandon as his face lit up with the glow from the fireworks. When we sat back up, the moment was gone, and we didn't even touch as we watched the finale in silence.

After he left and I'd gotten ready for bed, I lay wide-awake, staring at the ceiling. What the hell just happened? What did it mean? I tossed and turned until I gave up, made sure Mom was sound asleep, and then went into Tyler's room to write.

July 4th   Dear T—

The 4th just isn't the same without you. While I was watching the show, I was wondering what fireworks look like in heaven? I guess you look down at them, huh? Does it hurt the ears of kids who have died the way it used to hurt ours? You could probably get a nice aerial view and see them all across the country at the same time.

So Brandon came by tonight to watch the fireworks with me

How was I supposed to describe what happened between Brandon and me? Did I even need to describe it or was it only my runaway imagination pretending that Brandon would want to be with me? I stared at the open journal and started a sentence twenty different times in my head before stuffing the journal back into its hiding place.

Chapter Eleven

I texted Brandon before camp. I needed to know if what happened last night was for real. Brandon apologized. He admitted that he was drunk and that he felt bad for taking advantage of me. I was like a sister to him, and he didn't mean anything by it. My heart broke. Did he not feel the intensity of our kiss? I didn't have the courage to tell him that I wanted that kiss and a lot more. I didn't say anything that I really wanted to say. I assured him that I'd never say anything to Crissy. If he could ignore the chemistry between us, I was sure I could too.

When I entered the JCC, Jake walked past and shot me a high-five. Perhaps forgetting the kiss would be easier than I thought, as my palm made contact with his.

At lunchtime, I followed the campers to the JCC cafeteria that was just like any school cafeteria: loud, crowded, and obnoxious.

"Lex!" I called across the room.

She waved me over to her table, far from the fray of students.

"I hate having to eat before gymnastics," I sighed, sitting down across from her on the aluminum bench that always froze my thighs like Popsicles.

"I don't think we work out so much as babysit," she said. My eyes followed Lex's as she looked around the room in disgust. I had to agree with her, as we watched a group of

110

seven-year-olds blow bubbles in their milk through straws stuffed up their noses.

"How are your other classes going?" I asked, biting into a cold, soggy hamburger smothered in fluorescent mustard and bright-red ketchup that bore no resemblance to the burgers at the Highway Diner on the Black Horse Pike.

"Fine. I don't like the art class they make me teach. Yesterday, I had a kid who glued his fingers together and started crying," Lex shrugged her shoulders while stabbing a huge pile of lettuce, the only thing that was on her plate. I wondered if she'd finished her burger before I sat down.

"Oh. yeah, lots of treasures come out of art. Let's see, walnut shells painted to look like skunks, pipe-cleaner flowers," I said remembering back to some of the silly items I used to bring home from camp.

"You got it."

I looked down at my hamburger then back at Lex's mountain of salad. "Are you a vegetarian?" I asked as though I had solved the mystery of the universe.

"Yup. Have been my whole life."

"I'm so sorry! I can get rid of this if it's grossing you out. It's pretty bad anyway."

"Don't worry about it. I'm used to people eating meat in front of me."

I swallowed what was left in my mouth and then used my napkin to hide the rest on my plate.

"I've noticed you teach a lot with Jake," I mentioned, hoping it came off sounding casual. Since she's a regular counselor and not in training, she snagged the co-ed teaching slot every Tuesday and Thursday — the teaching slot co-led by Jake. While they're overseeing graceful dismounts off the beam or double backflips on the mat, I'm stuck with playground duty.

"Jake? Why does everyone think he's so wonderful?" Lex scoffed.

"Are you kidding me? He's amazing! I saw him in the gym before I left last night. He was working out on the rings and wasn't wearing a shirt. I couldn't stop staring. I must have stood there for at least ten minutes."

"He's all right, I guess. I'll let him know you've been watching him."

"Don't you dare!" I screeched after Lex shot me a look that suggested she might actually say something. "Tell me about him, please," I whined.

"What do you want to know?"

"Everything you know."

"Geez ... well, he's only here for the summer. His folks own a beach home in Longport. What do you call that? A Shoobee? He lives in Philly and just graduated. I guess he has a gymnastics scholarship to Penn State and is either going for pre-med or pre-law. Pre-something, I can't remember. One of those 'I have a four-year degree that doesn't qualify me for anything unless I keep going to school' situations, blah, blah, blah."

"Wow." That was all I could muster. Jake might be a doctor someday.

I imagined walking the campus of Penn State with him, arm in arm as we rustled leaves with our feet, giggling and kissing as we strolled.

"Yawn!" Lex sighed, but I kept up my soft interrogation.

"Does he have a girlfriend?" I asked as we walked our trays to the garbage cans.

"I don't know. Why don't you ask him yourself?"

"Yeah, right, ask him myself," I laughed at Lex as I scraped the remains of dead animal off my tray and wondered if I should consider going veggie myself.

As I was leaving camp for the day, I saw Jake again in the gym. The hallway was vacant so I stopped to watch through the narrow pane of glass in the gym door. Only a minute, I told myself, but I couldn't take my eyes off his body. As he held himself on the rings, every muscle was perfectly formed and knew its role in keeping him balanced.

Penn State. I could picture him there, competing at the college level. I imagined myself cheering from the stands as he nailed his dismount and struck his victory pose.

Suddenly, he really did dismount and we made eye contact through the glass. His look blossomed into a brilliant smile that made his eyes sparkle, and he was all gleaming white teeth and dimples. Reaching for a towel, he wiped off his face as he walked toward where I stood. My heart raced and I was surprised to find myself opening the door and walking into the gym.

"Nice job," I said. I did my best to sound all cool and casual like I always hang out after work watching hot guys practice.

I got a fresh smile as a thank you and blushed in reply.

"I saw you there yesterday." His soft brown eyes bore into me as his smile grew wider. My knees were shaking and my stomach clenched into a tiny knot. We're both counselors, I reminded myself, there's no reason we can't talk.

"You're good."

"I do what I can," he said in a quiet tone, still walking toward me. I thought of how someone was described as being coy in the issue of Seventeen I was reading at Louise's office, and realized that Jake's look was what the article was talking about. Jake draped the towel around his neck and reached his hand out to shake mine. Distracted by his sweat-soaked tank top and strong thigh muscles bulging out of his short shorts, I missed and my hand went off into space instead of connecting with his for a shake. Like a true gentleman, he didn't call attention to my idiocy.

"You're Kit, right? Lex's friend. I'm Jake." This time, he reached both hands to clasp one of mine into a hand sandwich. My mouth hung open. He knew my name. He knew I was friends with Lex. What else did he know? Had he actually been asking people about me?

"Yeah, I know," I answered, my voice nearly breaking.

"Kit's such a cool name. Is it short for something?"

"Katrina. But I hate being called that."

"Do you wear contacts? Your eyes are super cool green."

"What?" I stammered. Contacts? Really? "No, they're just my eyes." He noticed my eyes!

He nodded. "Say, you're a gymnast, right?"

I nodded yes.

"You should come by and work out with me sometime. I'm here practicing every day after camp. I could spot you."

My legs quaked. The thought of Jake spotting me, gently touching my back as I did a back walkover on the beam or supporting my legs as I went for a dismount on the uneven bars — it was too much to even think about!

"Umm ... okay." Don't stammer like an idiot, Kit!

"So maybe I'll see you around," he sort of half-asked, half-instructed as he turned and walked back to the rings. I was mesmerized as he easily tossed the towel on an empty chair before running toward the vault and hitting a perfect 10.

✱ ✱ ✱ ✱

"Honey, I'm home," Mom called from the back door.

I'd been home for about an hour watching a horror movie on TV, but as soon as I heard her voice, I changed the channel. Tyler and I were never allowed to watch horror movies, and I assumed that rule hadn't changed.

"Can you help me bring in the groceries?"

"I'll be right there," I groaned, peeling my tired body off the couch.

"Oh, Kit, where are your shoes?" Mom scolded, as I stood barefoot in the driveway.

"I'm fine. Where's Dad?"

"He's not coming home tonight; now go put your shoes on."

"Where is he going?" I asked, while Mom stuffed my arms with paper bags.

"He went to Philadelphia for the night to visit Ray. They're going to a Phillies game, I think. He'll be home tomorrow."

"That's strange. He never stayed out overnight before."

"Well, Louise says your father needs some space."

"Overnight in Philadelphia is a lot of space. It's only a half-hour away, forty-five minutes tops."

Mom gave me that look of hers. "Kit, go inside and put your shoes on right now!"

I took the groceries in and slipped on my flip-flops. By the time I was back outside, Mom had finished unloading the car.

"What's for dinner?"

"I thought we'd dig out that deep fryer you guys gave me last year for Mother's Day. I was thinking popcorn shrimp. I've always wanted to try making my own."

"Alright," I said, warily. Mom wasn't usually one for experimentation, which was why none of us were surprised the fryer was still in the basement, unopened, even though she'd been talking about wanting a fryer for years.

"Maybe if we get done with dinner early enough, we can head over to the theater and catch that new Will Ferrell movie. Lord knows I could use a laugh. Louise suggested it." Mom continued.

"Okay," I said with a mix of wariness and excitement as I went downstairs in search of the fryer.

We finished dinner early enough to catch the 7:30 movie. Mom laughed a lot, but in a forced, "Wouldn't this make Louise proud" sort of way that creeped me out and made me wish we'd stayed home instead and just watched TV.

"Let's walk on the boardwalk for a little while, shall we?" she suggested. The night was warm with a soft breeze, one of those nights I could have walked forever.

"Did you like the movie?"

Mom only nodded her head.

We walked along in silence and I wondered when I should start talking — and about what — but more than that, I wondered when she'd ever ask me anything about my life again.

"I love this island," Mom sighed after a few more blocks. Her tone was eerie, like she'd turned into some kind of ghost from the horror movie I was watching earlier, The Ghost Who Used To Be My Mom.

"Me too," I offered, not knowing what else to say.

"You know, I think this is the first time I've been on the boardwalk all summer. I don't even think I've gone to the beach once this year."

"Really? Well, let's go tomorrow. You can't go the whole summer without a tan," I insisted.

"Okay, we'll go tomorrow," but she said it in a way that I knew meant that we wouldn't.

Mom and I made it home in time for *The Late Show*. Neither of us mentioned how empty the house was without Dad ... and Tyler. As usual, Mom fell asleep halfway through and I helped her to bed when the show was over. Once I was sure she was asleep, I snuck into Tyler's room, and pulled out the lyric book.

July 5th

T.

Surprisingly enough, Mom and I actually had a good night. I almost forgot that Dad's, well, wherever he is. He barely even talks to me anymore. He's spending more and more time with Brandon, though. I'm trying hard not to let it get to me, but honestly, it's like he wishes Brandon was his son and that I would disappear.

Brandon and Dad went sailing last weekend and they're gearing up for the Atlantic City race next month. Dad's all excited. He's even making new crew shirts. He still won't let me crew with him. He says it's a guy thing on the boat and I'd just get in the way. I think he never got over that time I got seasick on the way to Steve's place in Cape May.

Anyway, Mom and I had a great time tonight. We made some awesome fried shrimp. She finally pulled the fryer out of the box. Can you believe it? Then we saw the new Will Ferrell movie. I didn't mention to her how badly you wanted to see it. I tried not to think about that myself. It was good to hear her laugh again. Mom fell asleep in the middle of The Late Show. I don't think she's ever seen it all the way through. I practically had to carry her to bed. She hasn't made it to the beach all summer, so I'm going to try and drag her out tomorrow, but I'm not holding my breath.

I've been dying to tell you about how I like this guy at camp named Jake Sykes. Isn't that a great name? He's amazing on the rings. He thinks my name is cool and that I have great eyes. Lex knows him pretty well but she's no help when it comes to these things. I wish you could coach me on what to say or do.

Well, I'm getting sleepy, too. Geez, it's already 12:30. I'll write more later.

Your big sis,
Kit (Yes, I came out a whole six seconds first and don't you ever forget it!)

Chapter Twelve

It was Beach Day with the JCC, and Lex and I had spent the last half-hour trying to help a bunch of five-year-old girls build a sand castle. They were working too close to the water's edge so the waves kept demolishing them. Each time we tried to get them to move, they pitched a piercing group temper tantrum so we left them to figure it out on their own.

"Let's see what Jake's up to?" I suggested, and Lex rolled her eyes at me. I scanned the beach but didn't see him anywhere. Then I looked out over the ocean and saw a group of counselors playing beyond the breakers. I spotted Jake, but he didn't see me.

Lex and I began to walk back to the mess of towels, coolers, and toys, but on our way we noticed some commotion under the boardwalk. When we got close, we found eight boys playing underneath. There were strict rules that the boardwalk was off-limits, but this group always thought they were above the rules.

"Alright! Everyone out!" Lex's voice boomed and the little ones scattered like roaches. The older ones weren't so quick to go though and began an annoying rendition of "Why?" and "That's not fair!" and "But my mom lets me!"

"There's broken glass under there and God knows what else. Everyone back toward the water." I said, trying the rational approach, but Lex yelled another "Get out!" over me, made an aggressive move toward them, and even the older kids started running away.

"I think the Lisas are taking more than their share of time in the water. We've been on beach watch since lunch!" I whined to Lex while wiping sweat from my brow and looking longingly at the ocean. The sand was burning my feet and I danced in place, trying to find my flip-flops, which must have gotten buried somewhere near my towel, which was somewhere in our group's mess.

"Yeah, but remember last week? Sherry left the Lisas out to dry and they got zero time in the water?"

"Oh, you're right."

"Speaking of Sherry ...," Lex said, spotting Sherry a good way away from the mess. I finally found my flip-flops so Lex and I walked over to hassle her. She was sound asleep on the only beach chair in sight, a book cracked open lying across her chest.

"I didn't realize we got paid to sleep on the job!" Lex chided really, really loudly.

"Yeah, I had it all wrong. What the heck have I been doing?" I shrugged my shoulders and exchanged a knowing look with Lex. Sherry didn't lift her eyes, but mumbled "Go away" under her breath.

Bored with taunting Sherry, we kept walking down the beach.

Closer to the pier, a bunch of older boys were poking sticks at a stranded jellyfish. As Lex and I approached, we saw Jake and a couple of other counselors scolding them. By the time we arrived, the boys were getting a lecture from nerdy Ted. It didn't seem to be working very well though, so Jake stepped in, shirtless and still shaking the water from his hair. I tried not to let my drool show.

"So you guys have never heard the starfish story?" Jake asked.

I loved the starfish story. My grandma used to tell it to me when we'd go for walks on the beach.

"It's a classic," Jake continued. "There once was an old man who lived by the shore. Every morning at dawn, he would take a walk along the water's edge. One morning, he noticed something strange in the distance. The day was foggy, but he thought he could make out the form of a man dancing. The old man couldn't understand why someone would be on the beach that early and especially why he'd be dancing."

A few of the boys snickered. I couldn't take my eyes off Jake's perfect lips.

"Okay, you jerks, keep listening. As the old man walked closer, he realized it was actually a woman, not a man, and she wasn't dancing at all. She was throwing something into the water. When he reached her, he saw that she was picking up starfish and tossing them into the ocean. 'Why are you throwing starfish into the sea?' the man asked.

'The tide is going out and the sun is rising and the starfish that are left on the beach will die,' the woman answered, never stopping what she was doing.

'But that's such a waste of time and energy! There are so many starfish and there are miles and miles of beach. What difference does it make?'

"The young woman reached down for another starfish. 'It makes a difference to this one,' she said as she threw it far out into the sea and moved down the beach."

Jake left a dramatic pause at the end.

"And the moral of the story is ...?" Jake waited for one of the boys to say something, but no one said anything.

"These jellyfish are like the starfish in the story," I called out. "Saving one is as important as saving them all." Jake's eyes fixed on me, sparking a shiver up my spine that tingled down my arms.

"I was hoping one of you little twerps would answer," he said, pushing two of them onto their backs in the sand. "Kit's right. These jellyfish are like the starfish. They're living things. You wouldn't treat your dog that way, so don't hurt the jellyfish. Maybe you're not going to pick them up and send them back to the ocean, but you don't have to torture them any further." The kids walked away, heads hung in silence, while I stood, feet locked in place, staring at Jake until Lex shook me back into reality.

* * * *

I got home with barely enough time to shower and change before Lex and Brandon came over. They were meeting each other for the first time, and I was nervous that it wouldn't go well.

"So, how long have you been in Margate?" Brandon asked Lex as we left my house and walked to the jitney stop. We were headed to the rides on Steel Pier and the jitneys, our little busses, were the best way to get across the island.

All day, I tried to put Tyler out of my mind. The thought of going to the Pier, to the rides, without him, the idea of having fun when he couldn't … well, I just couldn't think about it.

"Not long," Lex sighed.

"Oh," Brandon nodded, looking to me for help. Perhaps I didn't explain Lex's moods and quirkiness well enough. "Do you like it?" Brandon tried again.

"It's fine."

"Kit says you're really awesome at gymnastics."

I smiled at Brandon. He was such a good sport.

"Yeah, I am," she said.

The jitney pulled up right as we got to the stop. We followed each other on, dropping in our fare for the ride to Atlantic City. Brandon stopped asking questions and the three of us rode the whole way in silence.

Being that it was the height of tourist season, the pier was packed with people.

"I need to find a bathroom," Lex said. "Wanna come?"

"I'm good. I'll hang here with Brandon."

Lex sighed as she walked away.

"What a bitch!" Brandon said as soon as Lex was out of earshot. "This is your new friend? Geez, Kit!"

"She's not that bad. You just need to get to know her." Brandon gave me that look that said I'd lost my mind. Maybe I had. "I'm serious! I thought she was a little weird at first, too."

"That's more than weird," he cringed.

"Brandon, please!"

"Besides, I don't get the sense that she's going to let me get to know her."

"At least she isn't fake. That's more than I can say about some of the people you choose to spend your time with."

"Don't you dare talk bad about Crissy," Brandon threatened but then dropped it. "Kit, you can find better friends than her."

And you can find a better girlfriend than Crissy, I wanted to add but didn't. After that night in the attic, everything seemed a bit more taboo and what I'd once teased about now had a new seriousness. If I'd said it, would I have been implying that I would make a better girlfriend? Of course I would, but Brandon's my friend and we already went there and he made it clear he wasn't interested. And then there's Jake. Ah, to hell with it all.

"We have to ride the roller coaster at least once," Lex smiled as she returned from the bathroom and walked confidently up to the ticket booth. I looked out over the ocean, wishing I could fly away with the seagulls.

"No roller coaster," Brandon insisted.

"Why even come here if you're not going to ride the roller coaster?" Lex demanded, thrusting out her hip.

"Kit won't go," Brandon answered for me. I was still staring off to sea, ignoring them. "She puked over the side when she was a kid, and she hasn't been on one since," he explained to Lex like I wasn't standing right there beside them.

"Oh, come on, you're not a kid anymore. Bet you'd do it if Jake were here!" Lex taunted.

"Shush!"

"Who's Jake?" Brandon asked. I sensed a hint of jealousy and my face flushed.

"No one," I snapped.

"Right, no one," Lex laughed.

I shook my head, refusing more information, but I could feel Brandon's stare.

"Let's go," I said and they both began walking away from the ride. "No," I corrected, "this way." I said, making sure they were following me to the end of the line for the coaster.

"See!" Lex cried.

"Don't worry about it, Kit. No one's going to pressure you into going," Brandon assured me while glaring at Lex.

"No, it's a stupid fear and I'm ready to go. Let's just do it." I started thinking of all the things that Tyler wouldn't ever get to do again, and somehow it made me want to push myself and do things I never would have normally done, like I was doing it for him. But really, I was doing it for me.

The line was super long and my legs quivered in anticipation as we waited. The butterflies in my stomach made me wish I hadn't eaten that extra piece of pizza at dinner. Ten minutes later, the attendant emptied out one of the cars and we slid in. I sat between Brandon and Lex, hoping like hell that I wouldn't need to puke again.

The coaster started to creak its way along the tracks. I wasn't prepared for the side-to-side movement that made it feel like it could shift right off the track and topple over the side. I wondered if it would be worse to close my eyes or watch the people on the pier as they got smaller and smaller as we climbed higher and higher. The coaster began to climb and Lex and Brandon each took one of my hands and held on tight. I thought of Tyler as we chugged our way up, like we could keep going right up to heaven.

I had just lost myself in the idea of heaven, Tyler, and escape when the coaster crested and we plummeted toward the pier; my stomach clenched, and my heart jammed against my ribcage. I closed my eyes and held on as Lex and Brandon screamed in joy with the others on the ride. The ride slowed to a stop and it took all of my energy to move my rubbery legs out of the car. I did it! I told myself. And I'll never do it again!

"So?!" Lex started, dying for me to join her in her excitement.

"Sorry." I looked at Lex, sure that my face was white and the puke would come any second.

"You were a trouper," Brandon smiled, rubbing my arm.

"Let's go find a ginger ale or 7-Up before I get sick."

After my stomach settled down, we rode the Tilt-a-Whirl and the Swings, and then I made them ride my favorite, the Scrambler, three times. Nothing beat the one at this pier because it was set up so you actually swung out over the ocean on one of the spins.

By the time we got to the glass house, Brandon and Lex were joking with one another. They seemed to have bonded over their love of the roller coaster.

"Anyone up for some Skeeball before the pier closes?" I asked.

Brandon rolled his eyes at me.

"Sure," Lex said, which in her language was a resounding yes.

I beat everyone at Skeeball. I swear it was in my genes, the knack for knowing exactly how to land the ball in the 50-point ring. Tyler was the same way. Brandon left Lex and me at Skeeball as he headed for the shooting gallery, and came back about fifteen minutes later with a stuffed rabbit.

"Did you win that for Jason?" I asked, laughing at the enormity of the toy.

"No. I got it for you," Brandon said, handing me the rabbit. "Keep him in honor of riding the roller coaster. Tyler would be proud."

I hugged Brandon and started to cry. He started tickling me and I began to laugh uncontrollably. He leaned over and whispered in my ear, "I don't want to see you cry tonight."

I smiled back at him, and he tickled me some more.

"All right, kiddies," Lex jumped in, spoiling the mood. "I need to get you guys home. It's approaching Kit's curfew." I looked at my watch and realized I had twenty minutes before Cinderella time. If we caught the next jitney, I just might make it, so we made a mad dash for the closest stop.

It was still ten minutes before curfew when Lex got off at her stop. I waved goodbye with one of the rabbit's feet.

"Thanks for Fluffy," I said to Brandon while hugging the stuffed animal tight.

"No, you can't name him Fluffy."

"Oh, yes I can!"

"I'll take him back and give him to Jason."

"You wouldn't do that," I pouted.

"Oops! Your stop, my lady," he said in a fake British accent.

"Goodnight, sir," I said, standing up to leave.

"Goodnight, my fearless creature." He smiled brightly and kissed the back of my hand. As I got off the jitney, my heart raced a little.

When I got to my room, I found a package on my bed from Grandma. Inside was a super old-looking book called Many Mansions by someone named Edgar Cayce. It had a musty smell, like it had been there on Grandma's shelves forever. Tucked inside the book was a handwritten letter on

Grandma's yellow stationery. Just seeing the color of the paper got me excited.

Dear Kit,

May this be the beginning of your spiritual journey! This world we live in is but an illusion and I'm proud of the steps you've taken to learn more of this for yourself. I thought I'd start you off with this book, one of my favorites. It's a wonderful primer on spirituality and reincarnation, and the author, Edgar Cayce, is near and dear to my heart.

I hope things are going well for you and that you're able to find some joy in your life. Are you still seeing Louise? Do write when you can. I'd love to hear from my special Kit.

All my love,
Grandma

I opened the book and began to read.

Chapter Thirteen

I woke to the sound of a lawn mower outside my bedroom window. Holy crap! Ten o'clock! I didn't even remember falling asleep, and there I was, still dressed from yesterday and my face smashed into Grandma's book. I pushed myself out of bed, opened the curtains, and saw Brandon in the backyard mowing our lawn.

Since Tyler died, Brandon had been coming over every Saturday morning to help out with chores. Sometimes, he and Dad went sailing when he was done, but today Brandon promised he'd hang out with me at the beach. I was sick of going alone. Lex never wanted to go. She thought it was boring to spend the day at the beach even though I tried to convince her that it was completely different from beach day with camp. The beach was the only place I felt at peace.

I put on my swimsuit, slipped on one of Dad's old boat shop T-shirts, and pulled my hair into a ponytail. In the bathroom, I splashed cold water on my face for good measure, trying to rub out the deep lines caused by falling asleep on the book. While I never normally wore makeup to the beach, I thought a little lip-gloss might be in order.

Downstairs, Mom was preparing the usual Saturday breakfast feast: eggs, sausage, pancakes, and fruit. As I entered the kitchen, she was standing at the stove, flipping pancakes. The room smelled like a bakery, and my stomach gurgled in response. When Mom wasn't in front of the TV, she was in front of the stove. She'd become like Linus from Peanuts, but her blanket was a stove.

"Smells great!" Brandon called as he came in the back door, sweating like crazy, his shirt sticking to his body, and the smell of fresh-cut grass hanging on him like sour cologne.

"Breakfast is almost ready. Go wash up, Tyler," Mom called. Brandon and I stared at each other. Mom turned to us with a look of horror on her face.

Brandon froze. He was as freaked out as I was. Mom started crying and muttering "Oh God, Oh God" over and over. I rushed to her side to give her a hug and, as sweaty as he was, Brandon did, too.

"It's no big deal, Mrs. Carlin," Brandon said as he hugged Mom. Looking past her shoulder, the look on his face told me it was anything but.

After a very quiet, uncomfortable breakfast, Brandon and I packed our backpacks with towels, sunscreen, Cokes, and water, and strapped our boogie boards to our packs. It was a typical, hot, muggy day — perfect beach weather. We staked out our usual spot on Huntington Avenue Beach and lay in the sun until we were so hot we couldn't stand it, and then we ran toward the water, diving in like torpedoes.

"These are awesome waves," Brandon called. "Race you to shore!" he screamed, but his body had already caught the next wave and he was gone before I could even turn around.

"Hey, I wasn't ready!" I screamed back before catching a wave and following him. We bodysurfed until we were thoroughly exhausted, then dragged ourselves back to our towels, and flopped down.

My mind had been abuzz all morning from Grandma's book, with thoughts of death and rebirth and the soul nagging at me.

"Do you believe in heaven and hell?" I asked as I drew circles in the sand with my finger and thought back to last night and the roller coaster to heaven.

"What?"

"Heaven and hell, what do you think?"

"Really, Kit?" Brandon lifted his head off his towel and looked at me like he was thinking, do we have to go there?

Yes, we do. We very much have to go there, I thought back. I desperately needed to talk, and Brandon was my designated listener.

"Last night when I got home, I had a package from my grandma and inside was a book on reincarnation. I stayed up really late reading it and made it like halfway through. It got me thinking about whether or not heaven and hell are actual places."

"You mean like physical places with real angels and devils?"

"I guess. That's what I'm wondering, really. Are these places real? And if they are, what are they like?"

"I don't know." Brandon put his head back down on his towel and turned to face the opposite direction.

"Come on. What do you think happens to people when they die? Where do they go?"

"I guess I don't think about it."

"Really? Don't you wonder where Tyler is, what happened to him?"

"He's dead," Brandon said, turning back to me. His words came out harsh and piercing. "That's what happened to him."

"Come on, Brandon," I begged. "Don't be a jerk about it. What happened to his soul?" I pressed the issue. "Have you ever thought about reincarnation?"

"Not really. I know I don't believe heaven is a bunch of angels with wings flying around, or that you spend your days lying on clouds drinking lemonade."

"Lemonade?"

"I guess that somehow seems like an angelic drink." Brandon's serious tone, mixed with my own jangled nerves, caused me to start laughing uncontrollably.

"Why not milk?" Brandon threw a handful of sand at my elbow.

"Wait! Maybe angels drink Gatorade!" I said through fits of hiccupping laughter. Brandon's dimples were full-blown and a weird little jolt went through me as I watched him pretend to be upset.

"So what do you think?"

"Okay," I said, taking a deep breath. "So I think he didn't die. I mean his soul, not his body. Maybe he's here watching us right now."

"Stop it. You're wigging me out." Brandon craned his neck around as if he thought Tyler's soul was hovering somewhere close by, the way I did when I was walking with Grandma during shiva.

"Are you ready to go back in the water?" I sat up and wrung out my sticky ponytail, which was now all knotted and crisp from the saltwater. I cursed myself for being too lazy to braid it.

"Yeah, sure," he said, standing up. "Race ya?" But by the time I got up, he was already halfway to the water.

Brandon and I were playing sharks and bait when I felt something brush across my arm. I shooed it away and then looked in the water as jellyfish tentacles drifted by. Within seconds, the sting set in and I was bellowing from the bottom of my gut.

I swam out as fast as possible, considering my arm felt like it was going to fall off, and raced to the lifeguard stand.

"I got stung!" I screamed at the lifeguards.

"Hose it off," one of them said flippantly, reminding me that this was a regular occurrence at the shore. He pointed at a hose under the stand.

Brandon was right behind me and heard the lifeguard. Grabbing the hose, he sprayed down my arm.

"Isn't there something you can do? I'm dying!" I screamed up to the stand. The water wasn't doing a thing.

"Urine works."

"What?"

"If your boyfriend pees on your arm, it will take the sting away." The lifeguards started laughing and Brandon turned beet red. I wondered if he was more embarrassed at the thought of peeing on me or at being called my boyfriend.

"You creep!" I yelled at the lifeguard.

"Your call, but that's what works."

I started wailing like a baby, half-screaming, half-crying. Brandon watched in horror as though my arm had fallen off and was now spouting blood.

The lifeguards looked at Brandon with pity.

"Your girlfriend's pretty feisty," the other guard said.

"He's not my boyfriend!"

Brandon looked toward the stand and shrugged his shoulders.

"Good thing for you, eh, bud?" he winked at Brandon.

"I should get our stuff and call your mom," Brandon said in a hushed tone.

"Okay," I relented, grabbing the hose from him and hosing my arm off with my non-injured arm. "How long before it stops hurting?" I called to them.

"Probably won't go away until the morning," the first one replied coldly, not even looking in my direction.

"You're kidding!" The pain was unreal. How was I going to make it through the night?

"Stings take a while to wear away. My best advice is to load up on painkillers and go to bed."

I'd lived on the shore my whole life and had never been stung. Now, there I was, a fifteen-year-old local, crying to the lifeguards like a scared tourist.

"Your mom's on her way," Brandon said as he came running back with our stuff. "We can get your bike in her trunk and I'll ride home."

"Okay," I nodded.

"Thank you," Brandon called up to the lifeguards. They waved a hand at us without turning around.

"Let me help you up to the boardwalk," Brandon said, draping my non-stung arm over his shoulder and supporting me as we walked across the hot sand.

"I'm so embarrassed."

"Don't be. I get stung every few years. It totally sucks. I know how you feel."

I smiled at him and he pecked my check as we climbed the stairs to the boardwalk. We waited on a bench until Mom arrived. I played up the pain even more to have an excuse to leave my head on Brandon's shoulder. He rubbed my hair and I closed my eyes, pretending he actually was my boyfriend and not just a friend. Mom showed up faster than I expected, and I was actually sad to go.

"I'll give you a call and check on you later," Brandon squeezed my good arm as he buckled me into Mom's car.

"Thanks for everything."

Brandon smiled before loading my bike in the trunk and then riding off on his own. When I got home, Mom gave me part of one of her Valiums and I drifted off to sleep.

Chapter Fourteen

It was a rainy Saturday afternoon, and Brandon and I were being total couch slugs watching a Japanese monster movie. The weather report had said a bad gale storm was coming, sort of like a light hurricane. Warning notices started flashing across the bottom of the screen that the massive storm would make landfall soon. It hadn't reached a hurricane category yet, but they thought it might by the time it made land. I picked at my cuticles.

Right when the evil Japanese dragon bit the head off the damsel in distress, Brandon's dad called into the room and we both jumped three feet off the couch.

"Brandon, it's getting pretty bad out. I want the television unplugged."

"Okay, Dad." Brandon rushed to the set to unplug it as a bolt of lightning touched down across the harbor.

"Kit, call your Mom and tell her you're going to ride out the storm here. It's getting bad enough I don't even want to drive you home in this. Brandon, I need you to help me bring in the deck furniture."

Brandon went out on the deck with his dad while I called Mom to tell her I wouldn't be home. She'd assumed as much, although I hated that she was alone. Where the hell was Dad? I hung up and joined Brandon and his dad on the deck.

Brandon lives on the back bay, so his deck is literally right above the water. The sea spray pummeled us and the saltwater stung my eyes. The horizon was pitch black. Brandon and I exchanged a worried look. The ripping wind and splashes of water gave me goosebumps from head to toe. Maybe it wasn't tank top and short-shorts weather after all.

Back inside and from the kitchen window, we looked out over the bay and watched as the pounding waves rhythmically smashed their speedboat against the dock. The boat hung suspended on two poles above the water, right at deck level. The waves were vicious in their assault, as though they were trying to take the dock and the boat out to the sea.

"That boat's not gonna make it ..." Brandon's mom said wistfully. "Honey, sweetie, why didn't you dry dock the boat at Matt's place?"

I loved to hear Brandon's mom talk. Although she'd been living in New Jersey for nearly twenty years, she never lost her thick South Carolina accent. Her soothing voice always made the worst of problems seem like mere pinpricks.

"All the weather reports said that this was headed further north."

"There go our insurance premiums," she sighed, but in her sing-song voice it almost sounded like it wasn't a big deal. "Oh, and don't look at me with that mischievous smile, James. I know how badly you wanted a new boat." Only Brandon's mom called his dad by his full name. Everyone else called him Jim.

"Let's say it's God's way of telling me I deserve a new boat," he winked at Brandon and me. Brandon's folks were so carefree with one another. They were always kissing and hugging. If this conversation had been happening at my house, Dad would have already left.

The waves were now crashing over the deck. We were in for the long haul. Brandon's dad got everyone going on a game of Monopoly, but it did a poor job of keeping our eyes — and our minds — off the storm.

As we were wrapping up the game, something exploded downstairs. All of us raced down and stared in disbelief. The first floor was covered in a foot of seawater and the sliding glass door was gone. Shards of glass glinted in the water.

"My room!" Brandon cried, lunging for the stairs.

"Oh, no you don't!" Brandon's dad pulled him back by his T-shirt. "There's broken glass everywhere. Get some boots or something to cover your feet." Everyone ran upstairs to find protective shoes. I felt stupid wearing his mom's winter boots but I couldn't wade through glass-filled seawater in my flip-flops.

We made a human assembly line up the stairs, pulling the most valuable items from the basement. Brandon's stereo was destroyed, along with his beanbag. Basically, anything that wasn't at least two feet off the ground was trashed. Brandon's *Rolling Stone* collection was stored in boxes under his bed. Ruined. Every time I tried to make eye contact with him, I couldn't. His eyes were glazed over in shock.

Cleaning up took most of the afternoon, and by the time we had salvaged what we could, the living room was a maze of stuff with thin walkways to the couch and kitchen. The storm had not let up and the driving rain was so loud we could barely hear each other.

"Kit, call your folks," Brandon's mom said, and I immediately thought, *"You mean call my mom? Because my Dad is AWOL."*

"This storm isn't gonna die down 'til well into the night. You'll have to sleep over."

The only bedroom on the main floor was Brandon's parent's room. I wondered exactly where Brandon and Jason and I would sleep.

I tried to reach Mom on the home number, but the lines were down, so I called her cell. She said the roads were so flooded that there was no way to cross the causeway.

* * * *

I spent most of the evening helping Brandon dry off what was salvaged from his room, which wasn't much. Poor little Jason was so scared by the storm that he opted to sleep in his parents' bed instead of in the living room with Brandon and me. We each took a section of the L-shaped couch. I tried to pretend we were having a fun campout, but Brandon was too devastated over his room to play along.

"You okay?" I squeezed Brandon's arm from where I lay on my couch. Our heads were nearly touching.

"I feel like there's a bad cloud hovering over me this summer," he said with his chin on his pillow and his eyes fixed on something in the distance.

"No getting depressed on me. It's just stuff. You can replace it," I said, trying to cheer him up.

"That's what I keep trying to tell myself." He sighed and flipped onto his back. "I should go find that flask of Jack Daniel's," he said, staring at the ceiling.

"Your parents are right down the hall."

"They're asleep. They won't know."

"Please don't." I immediately thought of Dad and his way of drinking to forget. "Have you drunk more of that since the funeral?"

"A few times."

"Brandon," I sighed, rolling over and reaching for his arm again. I thought back to his beer breath on the Fourth of July and was growing more and more worried that Brandon was headed down a bad path.

I felt a need to be close to him, more than I'd ever had before. "Alcohol isn't going to make the pain go away. It's not going to reverse time and bring Tyler back." I knew that I was being dorky-preachy, but I had also struck a nerve. It was dark in the room, but I could tell he was crying. I got up from my side of the couch and kneeled on the floor next to him. I wanted to hug him and rock him like Tyler used to rock me when I had nightmares.

Grabbing his hand, it shook in mine as tears streamed down both of our faces.

"Why did he leave us?" Brandon choked out between sobs. "That son of a bitch! Why did he have to die?"

I clung hard to his hand and then pulled myself up so that I was lying on the couch next to him. Both of us shaking and crying and generally falling apart. Brandon threw his arms around me, gripping tight to me like a buoy in rough water. We lay together sobbing, and I felt safe in his arms, happy and loved. Brandon moved back after a bit and propped his elbow up so that he could look me in the face. We stared at each other for what felt like forever before he pulled me close, kissing me urgently on the mouth. Our lips remained locked as we held each other tight. I thought back to the attic and our first kiss. Through his lips, he was telling me how desperately he needed me. Could you say *I love you* with your lips?

Brandon's hands rubbed my back and wiggled their way up, underneath my top. I moved back a bit from his hold so that his hands could move to the front, my breasts aching to be held in his hands; every piece of me aching to be as close to him as possible. I felt the grief give way to pleasure, and I just wanted to be happy again. Brandon let his fingers search under my tank top until his hand entirely covered my left breast. He was gentle as he massaged it, lightly playing with my nipple and causing an intense pulsing sensation between my legs. I wished he'd put a hand down there, too.

I let my hands search under his shirt, moving over his arms, down his chest, and feeling the indentation of his belly button. This was as far as I'd ever gone with a guy before. Second base. I'd never let my hand go into a boy's pants, and a boy's hand had never gone into mine.

What does this mean? Could this really be the start of us? Crissy raced into my mind and I pushed her away. He wanted me now.

Then we heard a noise.

"What was that?" I asked, as I pulled my shirt down.

"It sounded like Jason." Brandon quickly pulled away from me.

"Brandon," Jason called from down the hallway. "Brandon," he repeated as he got closer. I jumped over to my side of the couch and pulled the blanket tight around me. Brandon sat up and peered down the hall.

"What's up?" Brandon asked as Jason came into sight, feet shuffling and blanket slung over his shoulder.

"Dad's snoring and I can't sleep. Can I sleep with you?"

"Sure," Brandon said, making space for Jason on the couch beside him. The space I was just in.

"Good night, Kit," Jason sang as he nestled in next to his brother.

"Good night, guys," I said, my eyes searching for Brandon's, but they were already closed.

Chapter Fifteen

Monday and Tuesday went by and Brandon and I still hadn't spoken. I'd started several texts, deleting each one. Things couldn't just go back to normal after that night at his house, could they? Since he was the guy, shouldn't he contact me first? I knew we were playing a stupid game of chicken, but I didn't have the guts to initiate, so I neurotically checked my phone every five minutes, hoping he'd written something. Anything.

Wednesday afternoon started off with another shift of playground watch at camp. I stood under the shady branches of a maple tree, trying to avoid being pulled into a game of "Let's Pretend." I stared at Sherry, my playground watch partner, as she leaned against the aluminum fence, deeply engrossed in a romance novel. She always had one with her, as if she was above actually working Sometimes you could even hear her moan when she read a racy part — so gross!

"Kit! Come down the slide with me," Sophie tugged at my shorts, looking up at me with her big brown eyes, her strawberry blonde ringlets framing her face. Sophie had latched onto me so much that her parents began asking me to babysit. It was nice to have extra money and a good excuse to get out of the house. I followed Sophie up the slide, judging that if I landed just right, I could "accidentally" shower Sherry with dirty playground sand.

Sherry was engrossed in the same book she'd been carrying all week, *Fairplay Faraway: The Seduction of Francine*. It must have been an alphabet-series book because I swear last week's title was *Eleanor something or other*. Every few moments, she'd wave the book like a fan to cool off.

From the top of the slide, I spotted Tyler's girlfriend Melissa walking on the opposite side of the street. I hadn't seen her since the funeral. She was holding hands with some guy, but I couldn't make out who it was. I forgot Sophie was behind me as she dropped her hands over my eyes.

"Guess who?!" she squealed.

"Not now, Sophie!" I snapped, pulling her fingers away and looking for Melissa. Sophie howled like I'd stabbed her, while Sherry calmly glanced up from her book.

"What have you done now, Katrina?" Sherry huffed, crossing her arms. When I looked for Melissa, she was gone.

"That little bit...," I started to curse, but caught myself in time. I could only imagine the trouble I'd get in if Sophie and her friends went around repeating that word all day.

"Somebody ruffle your feathers?" Sherry sighed in a bored tone before burying her face in the book again.

"I don't believe it, I don't believe it," I repeated over and over.

I'd forgotten I was still sitting atop the slide when a chorus of kids began screaming behind me, "Go! Go! Go!" I turned around and saw Sophie biting her nails and looking scared.

"Believe what?" Sherry sighed as she flipped to the next page.

"That was Melissa, my brother's girlfriend. She was holding hands with some guy. How can she be with someone else already?"

"Your brother's dead. He doesn't have a girlfriend." Her bold statement, so raw, sent my heart plunging to my stomach. The next thing I knew, I flew down the slide and shoved her, causing her to lose her balance.

"You are such a bitch!" I screamed as the kids surrounded us.

"Freak!" she yelled, pushing me back.

"Don't ever mention my brother again!" I pushed her and this time she fell to the ground.

"Whatever," she huffed, standing up, dusting herself off, and picking up her book.

"And my name is Kit, so stop calling me Katrina!" I spat the words in her face.

"Mrs. Meyers! Mrs. Meyers!" Sophie squealed from the top of the slide. Out of the corner of my eye, I saw the camp director jogging toward us. At the sound of Mrs. Meyers' name, we stepped away from each other.

"All right, who wants to explain what's going on here?" Mrs. Meyers demanded with her arms crossed and brow furrowed so tightly that it looked like her face might crack open.

"She attacked me, Mrs. Meyers ...," Sherry started.

"I didn't *attack* you," I said, drawing out the word "attack" to emphasize just how foolish she sounded.

"Okay, children, playground time is over." Mrs. Meyers gathered all of the kids and started to lead them away. For a second, I thought that might be it, but then she turned to Sherry and me. "I want you two in my office, pronto."

"But, Mrs. Meyers ...," Sherry started to whine. Mrs. Meyers shot her a look that shut Sherry up immediately.

Mrs. Meyers' secretary eyed us, then shook her head as if to say "You stupid girls" before opening the director's door.

"Mrs. Meyers hasn't come back yet. You two can wait in her office. I suggest you not continue your argument in there," she said before closing the door behind her. Sherry and I waited in silence, refusing to make eye contact. I looked around and made a mental note of everything I saw, as if I were taking inventory and would have to report on it all later: photo with husband and three kids, JCC, coffee mug, fake fern.

Mrs. Meyers walked in without making eye contact. "That was the most unprofessional thing I've seen in a while," she said as she took a seat and finally looked at us.

I'd never been in trouble before, never even been called into the principal's office. I was always the good kid.

"Quite frankly, I don't give a hoot what you were fighting about, but fighting in front of the children is completely disgraceful, and most certainly, inexcusable. I know you aren't even ten years older than the kids you supervise, but they look to you as adults and authority figures."

I wondered how many times she had to give this lecture each summer. Sherry was whiter than her normal pale complexion, something I'd never thought possible. It was like the girl got less tan as the summer went on.

"With your little stunt, you undermined any respect you may have earned this summer," Mrs. Meyers continued. "As of today, you are both suspended without pay. When — and if — you come back, will be determined after I talk with the other directors — and your parents. You may get your things and leave. You are excused."

This time Sherry didn't protest.

I knew I should apologize to Mrs. Meyers, but I couldn't bring myself to do it. I could apologize to Sherry, but that would only confirm that she was right. So, there I sat feeling pretty bad, but not willing to do anything about it.

Mrs. Meyers stood up from her chair and opened the door, and Sherry and I left.

I started riding my bike to Brandon's. The adrenaline from the fight seemed like enough of a boost to send me over the edge to finally confront him, but when I got there, he wasn't home.

Who's Melissa's new boyfriend? I texted before taking off for home. That should get a response from him.

Two blocks away from his house, my phone binged from my backpack.

Joey Scanlon. Thought you knew. I read as I pulled to the sidewalk.

YOU knew about this?! My fingers flew over the screen.

You KNEW and didn't tell me?!

Fourth of July Party. They were together. Guess they're an item now.

I put the phone back in my backpack and finished riding home. What the hell was happening? I dug out my phone. Brandon hadn't texted back.

Tyler's barely been gone two months. How can she do this to him? I wrote.

Maybe she was lonely? People do a lot of things they shouldn't when they're lonely …

The phone dropped out of my hand and hit the floor. I began to shake, and then the tears came and wouldn't stop. It boiled down to this. I was Brandon's loneliness distractor. I was only keeping him company until Crissy came back. I'd been played. I'd been such a fool. Such a hopeless, dumb fool. He'd never wanted me. He just wanted someone, and I was there. I powered off my phone, went upstairs, and took a long, long shower.

Dad came home an hour later and confiscated my phone, took away my computer, and like when I was a child, would have said 'go to your room', but I was already there in my pajamas. They could punish me all they wanted, but getting that text from Brandon was worse than anything Mom and Dad could ever think to lay on me.

My stomach was growling something fierce, but I didn't want to go down to face my parents and their lectures. I picked up Grandma's book and let myself get lost in it.

I must have fallen asleep because I woke up and the clock read 1:30. The house was quiet, so I snuck into Tyler's room and dug out his journal.

July 19th

Dear T—

Today sucked! I got in a fight with this evil witch named Sherry. She's another counselor at camp and a complete idiot. Then I end up getting kicked out of camp and now I'm grounded for who knows how long. I won't go into why I got in a fight. If you saw it, you already know, and if you didn't, you don't need to.

I really wanted to write about Brandon, but since I hadn't shared anything until now with Tyler, what was I going to write? I made out with your best friend, forced him to cheat on his girlfriend, and now I'm pissed because he's acting like a creep and I really want him to like me like he likes Crissy?

I thought about bringing this journal into my room but I feel like you're here when I'm writing on your bed. Aunt Deborah told Mom we should convert your room into a quilting room or something, that way the healing process will go much faster. Mom can't sew a button let alone quilt. I think Aunt Deborah needs to spend less time worrying about what we should do and more time with her own family! Ari's in Israel for a few more weeks.

Well, I should probably go to bed. I'm not sure what I'll do tomorrow since I'm not going to camp. Knowing Mom, I'll probably have a huge list of chores waiting for me when I get up. I miss you, bud. God, do I miss you.

Love ya,

Kit

Chapter Sixteen

As I expected, a nasty note from Mom was taped to the bathroom mirror.

> Kit,
> You're not to leave the house or use the phone. By the time I come home from work, I want the refrigerator cleaned and scrubbed, the basement straightened up, your room cleaned, both bathrooms sparkling, and a note of apology written to Mrs. Meyers. With any luck, you won't get fired. I've set up a meeting with Louise for you for tonight. If I find out that you went to Brandon's or otherwise left the house, there will be serious consequences.
> Mom

Welcome to Day One of being grounded!

By lunchtime, I had completed most of the tasks on the list, saving the bathrooms and basement for last — my two least-favorite chores. I started the letter to Mrs. Meyers four times before putting it down and digging out my unicorn

148

stationery box (that I'd had since I was nine) to write back to Grandma instead. Maybe I wasn't allowed to use any of my devices, but Mom didn't say anything about old-fashioned letters.

Dear Grandma,

Thank you so much for sending me "Many Mansions". You're definitely going to have to send me more books soon as I've nearly finished it! I love the ideas on reincarnation and even tried to talk to Brandon about them. He doesn't seem as interested as me, so that's been a little frustrating.

I guess I should tell you that I'm in trouble. I got in a fight. Well, it was more of an argument with a bit of shoving. It happened at camp with another counselor (her name is Sherry) who's a total snob and completely full of herself. She's kind of cold-hearted and her attitude set me off. It all started when I saw Melissa, Tyler's girlfriend, holding hands with some guy.

I can't bear the thought that people are moving on with their lives without Tyler. Then Sherry snapped, "Your brother's dead," and it was like flipping a switch in my brain and I lost it. But that seems normal to you, right?

Mom scheduled an appointment for tonight with Louise. I don't want to go. I don't see why I

have to be grounded. I think you would understand.
It's not like I do this all the time. I've never been in
a fight. Why couldn't Mom just care a little and
ask me for my side of the story for once?

On a happier note, I have a new friend at camp.
Her name is Alexa, but she goes by Lex.

Lex! OMG! I never told Lex what happened. She's probably wondering where I am. I can't even call her from the house phone because her number is plugged into my phone. I'm going to have to find myself a carrier pigeon.

Lex is totally different from anyone I've ever
met. She is always saying or doing her own thing
and doesn't care what others thinks. She says
she's that way because she's an Aquarius. Does
that make sense to you? I think I need an
astrology book next.

I hope life is good in Florida. I still want to stay
with you next summer. I hope that can happen, if
I'm not still grounded.

Miss you like crazy!
Love, Kit

All day long, the house phone had been tempting me to call Brandon. It was an old-fashioned kind, plugged into the wall, so without a digital memory there was no way Mom could see that I'd made a phone call. By mid-afternoon, I couldn't take it any longer. I decided to suck it up and call

Brandon's house. Even if Mom found out, at least I'd done everything else on her list. Maybe I could fake that it was an emergency and I had to call someone. I knew Brandon was coming over tomorrow to help Dad, and I didn't want our first awkward conversation to be in front of him.

I dialed and his mom answered

"Hel-lo?" Mrs. Garner sang into the phone.

"Hi, Mrs. Garner, it's Kit. Can I talk to Brandon?"

"Sorry, sugar. He left with Crissy an hour ago."

"Crissy?" My heart leapt to my throat and tears began pooling in my eyes. This wasn't happening.

"Why, yes, she came home a few days ago. Poor thing, she was just having a miserable time in Switzerland. I think she was missing Brandon just too much to be away. They haven't been apart in days."

Poor thing? Haven't been apart? No! No! No! This wasn't happening. How could she come back early? *Breathe deep*, I coached myself. No! I can't breathe deep. *Do the math*, I tasked my brain. *When did she come back and when did he stop texting? So it was true: he had only kissed me because he missed her. He never wanted to be with me. I was just a prop to occupy his time. Wait, isn't that a song lyric? I'm falling apart and Mrs. Garner's on the other end of the line.*

"Kit, are you there?"

"Yeah, sorry."

"Is everything okay? You don't sound so good, sweetie."

Maybe he was getting back his ring and explaining to her how he was in love with me. Maybe if I just gave him space, this would all turn out all right. I could still win in the end.

"I was hoping to talk to him," I quickly added with a finality in my voice. I had to get off the phone. "I'll call later," I started to hang up, but as I pulled the phone away from my ear, I heard her say, "Well, I'll tell him that you called."

"Please don't," I begged. "I'll just call later."

"Okay, then. You take care, sweetie."

"Thanks. You, too," I said and hung up. I ran directly into my room and dive-bombed my bed. I took the stuffed animal Brandon had won for me and repeatedly slammed it against the mattress, hoping to burst it into a cloud of tiny Styrofoam balls.

Mom came home at five o'clock, and said nothing except "Hi." I thought I'd at least get some acknowledgement that I'd done everything on her list, but she wasn't interested in any conversation. What was the point of doing everything on her list if she wasn't even going to notice? We drove to Louise's office in silence.

Thankfully, Louise wasn't running late, as she sometimes did, so there was no unnecessary waiting time with Mom in the lobby. Louise motioned with her arm as a cue for Mom and me to take a seat. "Good evening, Kit," she smiled at me. "I heard you had a rather interesting week."

I couldn't believe they'd already talked about me. My shock escaped as a muttered "Umm" in response. I don't know why, but I figured Mom wouldn't have told Louise what had happened until our session. Knowing they'd already talked made me feel like they were ganging up on me.

"Louise, Kit's not herself. She's doing all these bad things"

"Wait, all these bad things? What bad things?! I got in one fight. Big deal!"

"Oh, there's more than the fight." Mom started to raise her voice. "You don't leave notes when you go to a friend's house. You haven't been keeping up on your chores. We still have rules in our house. Or maybe you think you're above them?"

"Oh. Well, what about you and Dad? You take off all the time, and I never know where *you* are. Neither of you care about me or ask me about my life. Dad's hardly ever home and when he is he's drunk ..."

"That's enough, Kit!" Mom cut me off.

I looked to Louise for help. This was unbelievable.

"Let's go back to the fight. Kit, can you tell me exactly what happened?" Louise asked.

"From what Mrs. Meyers said ...," Mom started.

"No, Susan. I want Kit to talk first." I was surprised by Louise's abruptness with Mom and began to believe I stood a chance of making it out of there alive.

I recounted everything in full detail, forcing Mom to listen to my story. Finally.

"You see what I'm saying? This is embarrassing," Mom interrupted half way through, and I realized that her anger was really over the embarrassment of me, her daughter, getting into a fight. That's why I was in trouble. It was because I made her look bad in front of Aunt Deborah and the whole snobby JCC community.

Louise explained to Mom that what happened on the playground was most likely "nothing to be alarmed by, but quite normal given the excessive stress Kit's been under this summer due to Tyler's death."

She talked to Mom like I wasn't sitting right next to her. Louise offered to write a note to the camp explaining the trauma I'd been through and suggesting that I be allowed to keep my job. She said she'd done things like that in the past, and they usually worked. Mom seemed quite pleased by it all. It was amazing how her opinion could be so manipulated by Louise.

"So, does this mean I'm not grounded?" I asked Louise.

"That's for your mother to decide," she said.

I turned to Mom and raised my eyebrows, as if to ask for a reply.

"We'll discuss it later. For now, yes, you're still grounded."

Since we hadn't eaten dinner, we picked up some Chinese take-out and walked into the house just after seven o'clock. Unlike earlier in the summer, Mom stopped commenting on whether or not Dad was home or even coming home. She figured he wasn't and so did I. We both just counted on each other for dinner. Mom took her food into the living room, and assumed her usual spot in front of the TV.

"Can I have my phone back?" I asked as she sat fixated on a reality cooking show.

"Uh ..." she sighed. "Fine, yes, you can have it back."

"Thanks. Where is it?"

"It's in Dad's nightstand drawer. You can get it."

I went upstairs to their bedroom and pulled open Dad's nightstand. My phone was sitting on top of a pile of sailing and boating magazines. I took it back down to the kitchen and powered it on. The only texts were from Lex. Nothing from Brandon. Of course not. He was too busy making out with Crissy.

Perhaps it was the exhaustion of the day or the fact that I had my period, but after dinner, I went upstairs and completely collapsed on the edge of my bed, falling into a mushy heap of tears. How had my life gotten so messy so quickly? Perhaps writing to Tyler would help clear out the gunk in my brain and heart.

No. He didn't need to hear about all my problems. It's not like he could fix anything anyway. Nobody could. I curled up in bed with Grandma's book nestled under my chin and let myself be transported into other realities.

Chapter Seventeen

Louise's letter did the trick, and I was allowed back at camp the following Monday. There was only two days' suspension for both Sherry and me. It was Saturday and Brandon was on his way over to work with Dad in the garage. Finally, I'd have a chance to force him to talk to me.

"Hi, stranger," I smirked as I opened the door to let Brandon in. "What, you don't know how to use a phone anymore?"

"Maybe we can talk after I help your Dad."

"Yeah, I guess Crissy's been keeping you too busy to actually give me the time of day, huh?"

"She just got back," Brandon said, trying to avoid my gaze.

"Glad I could keep you entertained while she was gone."

"Don't be like this," Brandon begged.

"Asshole," I mouthed as I heard Dad approaching behind me.

"Brandon! There you are," Dad called. "Ready to get to work?"

Brandon smiled at Dad.

"Come on back!"

I stepped aside, but kept my glare aimed at Brandon.

This time I didn't wait for Brandon to go to the beach with me. I gathered my things and was gone within fifteen minutes. He knew where to find me if he wanted to talk.

Sure enough, about an hour later Brandon walked up to my towel. I was lying on my stomach, facing the ocean and dreaming of swimming away. I purposely wore my new bikini, but who was I kidding? I looked like a board next to Crissy. There was no way to compete and that's why I'd never tried before. Now, I was just a pathetic joke.

"Okay, I'm here. Let's talk," Brandon said, sitting down in the sand next to me. Neither of us removed our sunglasses.

"Thought you were helping my Dad?"

"I told him I had to leave early."

"Oh," I nodded, caught off guard. Had he actually made me a priority?

"I'm sorry I didn't get a chance to talk to you before Crissy came home."

"Didn't get a chance or didn't have the guts?"

"Touché. I didn't know she was coming back so early. She didn't either. There was an emergency with her Mom ..."

"I don't care."

Brandon just nodded.

"Did we have something going or not?" I asked just anxious to rip off the Band-Aid and get right to the pain.

I looked toward him. He shook his head no while looking down the beach, refusing to make eye contact.

"The kissing, the making out — that was all my imagination?"

"It shouldn't have happened. It was all a mistake. I took advantage of you. I was lonely."

"Lonely? That's what that was?" I demanded, propping myself up on one elbow. He still wouldn't face me.

"I was confused. I am confused. You're Tyler's sister. I made this promise that I'd protect you. It all just got so complicated."

"You did what? You made a promise to who? To Tyler? My Dad? You're not my guardian angel, Brandon! I'm just like Crissy or anyone else. If you like me, why don't you have the guts to 'fess up? Nobody protects me. I can take care of myself. I'm not a kid."

"Kit, Kit, Kit ..." Brandon let his head flop between his knees and shook it like a dog.

I waited, but there was only silence. I didn't stop waiting.

"I love you," I said, tossing out my whole heart for him to hug or stomp on.

"I don't like you that way. I was confused ..."

"You already said that, but I don't believe you."

"Will you let me finish?" he demanded.

I sat up and started picking at the dried sand between my toes.

"I miss Tyler and you and me. I miss our friendship and sometimes I think I'm going to go crazy from the pain. I start texts to him. I look for him in places we used to hang out. I feel like I'm going insane. Hanging out this summer together with you, well, it's been great, like that friendship can go on, but it's not right. Crissy's my girlfriend."

"I don't believe you."

"What don't you believe?"

"I think you really like me, but you're scared to admit it. I think it's Tyler who's in the way. He's always been in the way of us. I didn't realize it until this summer."

Brandon wouldn't respond.

"You just don't want to admit to the world that you'd choose me over someone beautiful and big-boobed and gorgeous like Crissy."

"That's so shallow."

"But it's true. You can kiss me in the secret of your home, or cry on my shoulder, but you can't announce it to the world. You're just a wimp!"

Brandon stood up and brushed the sand off his butt. "I gotta run."

"Yeah, of course you do." I huffed as I turned my cheek and laid it back on the towel. I closed my eyes, but all I could see was Brandon taking paper hearts with my name written on them and ripping them to shreds.

✳ ✳ ✳ ✳

Monday morning came and I agonized over how I was going to handle playground watch with Sherry. I figured if we kept to our own parts of the yard, set our own turf, we'd be okay. As I brought my group of kids across the street at 1:55, I swore I saw Jake hanging from the monkey bars.

"Jake?"

"Hey, Kit!" Jake smiled wide and I got all jittery. He was my antidote to Brandon.

"So, are you my new co-babysitter?" I asked, wondering why I hadn't picked a fight with Sherry weeks ago.

"For today, at least. I think they're trying to figure out schedule changes. Guess they don't want you and Sherry near each other."

"Probably a good idea."

"So what were you two fighting over anyway?"

"Oh, nothing."

"Nothing? Whoa! I think I'll steer clear of you!" Jake laughed from deep in his belly. A ripple ran through me and I noticed my words speeding up.

"No, I'm not crazy," I said, but without much conviction. "I don't want to go into it. So, anyway, Lex tells me you start Penn State in the fall, that you've got a gymnastics scholarship. That's terrific."

"Yeah, should be pretty awesome. Where are you going?" he asked. Surely he didn't think I was old enough to be in college.

"Oh, I'm still undecided," I lied.

"You're not starting in the fall? Are you taking a gap year in Europe?"

"Nah," I shook my head, thinking how funny it was to be surrounded by all these rich kids who assumed if you weren't starting college, you must be going to Europe. If I was actually graduating, Mom would make me work in the clinic with her or get some kind of job. I certainly wouldn't be dancing in a nightclub in Paris, living on wine and croissants.

"I'm going to work, save money, you know."

"Right on. Hey, I'm having a party at my house Friday night. I've told Lex about it, but maybe you could remind her again. You two should come. Everyone's going to be there." He squeezed my arm and held it. The gleam in his eye conveyed the potential of a make-out session. I thought about Brandon being back with Crissy and my stomach knotted. Jake was interested in me. What did I need Brandon for anyway? My days of being a dateless wonder were over.

"We will definitely be there," I said, even though I knew there was no way I'd convince Mom and Dad to let me go while I was pseudo-grounded. I'd escape if I had to. I wasn't going to miss Jake's party for anything.

"Jake! Jake!" A group of boys came running over to us; for a minute, I'd forgotten we were on playground duty and not a date. "Come play ball with us!" The ringleader bounced a basketball directly into Jake's hands.

"Sure. Holler if you need me, Kit," he called as he ran off with the boys.

After camp that day, I saw a text from Brandon wondering if I'd come over and watch "Survivor." Really? Like

159

just hang out and be friends, like it was nothing? I deleted it then grabbed a magazine, poured a glass of lemonade, and cued up the jukebox. It was time to zone out in the lounge chair.

✱ ✱ ✱ ✱

After intense pleading with Louise, I convinced her to talk to Mom and Dad about letting me spend the night at Lex's. Of course, what I didn't share with Louise was that from Lex's we were going directly to Jake's party.

I'd never been to Lex's house and was surprised to find crosses with Jesus on them in nearly every room and a shrine to the Virgin Mary over the fireplace. I sometimes forgot that Lex was Catholic; her house reminded me of how religious some families could be. Personally, I didn't know how Lex could stand it. Not to mention her aunt had covered the furniture in plastic and the house had a vague chemical smell that reminded me of a nursing home and made me slightly nauseous. I bet Lex's house never smelled like banana bread the way ours often did.

Her room was as sterile as the rest of the house, kind of like a hotel room. In the corner, I spotted a suitcase with T-shirts falling out onto the floor as if she'd recently arrived.

"Is this your brother?" I asked, picking up a weathered wooden picture frame on the dresser. The photo was of a lanky guy, probably eighteen or nineteen. He looked like a male version of Lex – dirty blond hair and squinty eyes – and just like Lex he had a smile that seemed to be covering up a lot of pain.

"Yup, that's him. That's the beach at Coney Island. He used to take me there on weekends."

"He's cute." I smiled and set the picture back on the dresser.

"Stay away."

"Come on! He doesn't even live here."

I picked up another picture. Her dresser was covered with frames on a sea of dust bunnies. "Are these your folks?" The picture was set in a swanky restaurant booth and the couple was dressed super nice. Lex and her brother definitely took after their father in the looks category. Their mom looked like a dainty fairy, almost not real.

"Yeah," she called on her way out the door. "I need to go brush my teeth, then we should get going."

I walked around her room, studying the other pictures of her brother and parents. Some of them showed all four together and they appeared to be a very happy, normal family. The pictures called up memories of my family: Mom, Dad, Tyler, and me. Like Lex, we were once a unit of four and now we'd been chopped up. I started to get teary-eyed, but stopped myself short. I couldn't cry in Lex's room. There was no way I was going to have bloodshot eyes for Jake's party.

I was in desperate need of a new outfit, so I'd gone shopping earlier in the day. I was excited to put on my new low-rider jeans, a shimmery copper-colored crop top — which I hoped would nicely accent my green eyes — and my new platform sandals. I made sure enough of my tan belly was showing to entice Jake to pay attention to me. Lex was wearing her trademark baggy purple camo pants with a lavender tank and sneakers. The girl was hopeless.

"That's not going to get you any guys," I warned her.

"I'm not out to get drunk idiots at a stupid party."

"Are you sure you wanna go?"

"No. But I know you do. Don't worry, I'll give myself an attitude adjustment before we get there."

We took the jitney up to Jake's end of the island and arrived around 10 o'clock. Before we turned the corner onto his street, we could hear music pulsing from his house. People were spilling out onto the porch and lawn, polluting the salty air with the stink of cigarettes and beer. Jake lived in one of those huge mansions along the beach that had a swimming pool right by the boardwalk. I could never understand why someone had a pool if the ocean was their backyard.

Even though Lex was older than me, we both looked much younger than everyone at the party and no amount of makeup could change that. As we made our way through the house, people were standing around laughing, dancing, and occasionally sloshing some of their beer on the hardwood floor, making it sticky and gross. We slunk our way through the crowd looking for Jake. I worried that we'd never find him in the sea of people. I couldn't imagine this kind of party at my house. How would he ever clean it enough so that his parents wouldn't ground him forever?

Slowly, we made our way to the back of the house, arriving in the over-crowded kitchen.

"One tequila, two tequila, three tequila, floor!" the group chanted. Lex and I watched as a strikingly good-looking blonde surfer guy poured a decent amount of a bottle of alcohol down someone's throat. Lex gave me her "I told you so" look, and I nodded back. We were in way over our heads. She'd been trying to tell me for days that this wasn't our scene, but I couldn't get the gleam of Jake's eyes out of my mind. Besides, I wasn't going to miss an opportunity to purge Brandon out of my system once and for all. The person in the chair stood up, shook his head like a dog who'd been swimming in the ocean, and stepped aside. It was Jake.

"Lex!" Jake called as he made his way through the crowd. "I'm so glad you made it. Oh, and there's my buddy Kit! Kit, with the gorgeous green eyes." He hugged Lex, then me, but when he hugged me, his mouth landed on mine and a wet, sloppy tongue slipped between my shocked lips. I'd dreamed of kissing Jake, but it wasn't a kiss so much as an unscheduled landing. I tried my best to kiss back, but he slipped and slid around my mouth like his lips were ice-skating for the first time. Then he leaned into my ear and whispered, "I'm really glad you came."

The moment I'd fantasized about had finally arrived. I wasn't sure my legs would hold me upright. Jake did like me! I wasn't just his buddy. When I smiled at Lex, her face wrinkled into a scowl. She was just jealous.

"Let me show you girls around," he slurred, resting his right arm on my shoulder and his left on Lex's. Lex rolled her eyes at me for like the millionth time, but I didn't care. I was with Jake and that was all that mattered.

Jake wandered around, leading us from room to room, as if we were his harem. Lex's danger looks started coming in rapid succession. I ignored her. When we reached the back porch, we discovered a hot tub overflowing with naked people. There were others vomiting off the side of the porch and all around the lawn, I spotted couples making out in dark patches of the yard.

"This is quite a party," Lex sort of complimented Jake, but looked at me with a desperate plea that I knew I needed to acknowledge. I made eye contact, raised my eyebrows at Lex, and then looked away. She could go home. I wasn't leaving.

"We didn't see your bedroom, Jake," I said. Lex's jaw dropped and I wondered how I could ditch her.

"You want to see my bedroom, do you?" His words were taunting and Lex threw his arm off her shoulder.

"You two finish your tour. I'll be on the front porch," Lex said. On the way back through the house, Jake popped the cap off a bottle of beer and handed it to me. Lex had already taken off ahead of us, so I tipped back the bottle and the next thing I knew we were in his bedroom, and I'd downed half the beer. Lex was extremely anti-alcohol, something we normally agreed on.

"So ...," Jake whispered as he came up behind me and wrapped his arms around my waist. I gulped my beer, hoping the coolness of it would overcome the disgusting taste and that the alcohol would calm my nerves. I was standing in Jake's bedroom, I kept telling myself — alone with him in his bedroom.

"I brought another for you," Jake pulled the empty bottle out of my hand and replaced it with a fresh one, while his free hand roamed up my tank top. We started making out, all sexy and intense.

While we were kissing, he took the beer bottle from my hand and held my wrists behind my back. He kissed my neck and pulled my shirt down to begin kissing my chest. It all felt a bit harsh, but maybe that was the beer and he was just so strong. He pushed my shirt up until my breasts were completely exposed. The cut of the top didn't allow for a bra. I never really needed one anyway.

"Whoa!" I laughed, but Jake wasn't laughing as he guided me backward onto his bed, keeping my wrists held tight, but now above my head. Straddling me, he held my legs with his strong thighs and unbuttoned, then unzipped, my jeans.

"You don't need to rush," I teased, but Jake just smiled wide and kept going. Next thing I knew, he'd freed my hands, my pants were at my ankles, he was unzipping his pants, and his thing was dangling inches from my mouth.

"Hey!" I screamed as I attempted to push him away, careful not to touch it. Jake was way stronger than me though, and I couldn't budge.

"Come on, sweetie. Just a little sucky for Petey," he begged, brushing his thing across my lips and squinting as he smiled. Those eyes that used to slide into sexy slits now appeared like the eyes of a venomous snake.

I didn't even comment on the name as I focused all my energy on trying to wiggle free. It was no use. Jake's firm grip was too strong and when Petey pressed my lips apart, I gagged back a barf.

164

"What's wrong, Kit? You're in my bedroom, like you wanted," he mocked, as if all of this was my idea, like I couldn't wait to get him in his room and give him a blow job.

I pushed harder, but he held me tighter.

"Get off of me!" I screamed, but he smiled and mashed his clammy lips against my mouth. I was about to relent and let him have his way when someone knocked on the door. A woman's voice sang "Where's my Jakey?" Jake flew off me and called back, "I'll be down in a minute, babe."

"Okay, I'll be in the hot tub. I've been waiting for you."

"Babe?" I demanded, hurriedly pulling up my pants and pulling down my top.

"It's no one." Jake said, slipping on his shirt. Before I could get out of there, he'd pinned me back on the bed and was hovering over me again.

"Come on," he said, with a new urgency to his voice. "Are you going to give me some?" He kissed me sloppily on the mouth and ran his hand over my tank top and across my chest. He was lying fully on top of me, his mouth sucking on my ear.

I bit his ear.

"Ow!" he yelled and rolled off.

I buttoned my pants, fixed my shirt, rushed out of the room, and flew down the stairs.

I found Lex sitting on the porch swing, engaged in what I could tell was a boring conversation with a very drunk guy.

"Let's go," I demanded as I grabbed Lex's wrist and dragged her off the swing. As we got to the end of Jake's block, we could see cop cars bearing down. They turned onto Jake's street just as we reached the jitney stop on the opposite block.

I barely said a word the whole jitney ride back to Lex's. She knew something had happened, and I'm sure at some level it was obvious, what with my disheveled hair and smeared makeup.

Thankfully, her aunt was already asleep, so Lex loaded up a tray with milk and Oreos and said it was picnic confessional time in her bedroom.

"Okay, 'fess up," she demanded as she pulled apart an Oreo and began licking the white center. "What happened in Jake's room?"

"I'm such a fool!" I buried my face into the extra pillow she'd left out for me.

"So what. What I want to know is are you okay?"

"Oh, yes," I said sarcastically. "I'm fine. Minus the sensation of Petey shoved against my lips."

"Petey?"

"Lovely name for a penis, eh?"

"Oh gawd!"

"Oh, yes. I am so naïve. No, I'm stupid! Totally stupid! I just wanted to make out. Why do we have to go from first base to home plate in one inning? I'd like to just linger at second for a while. Oh God, I miss Brandon."

"Brandon?" Lex raised an eyebrow.

"If Brandon hadn't been so definitive about us, I never would have been in this situation."

Lex's eyebrow was still raised. She'd stopped licking the Oreo.

"Last Saturday, Brandon and I had The Talk. We're officially not happening. He's one-hundred percent back with Crissy."

"Since when were you and Brandon an item?"

"I guess I never really shared that, huh?"
"Uh, guess not."

"We've kissed, made out a few times. I've had a crush on him forever, and I thought now my time had finally come. But he doesn't want me. I'm too much like a sister."

"Oh, right. Crissy's his girlfriend."

"Yes!" I cried as I wrapped my arms around the pillow and used it as a crash pad as I toppled onto the bed.

"I can't believe you never told me about you and Brandon," Lex said as she picked at a scab on her arm. Lex's body was covered in various cuts and bruises — the life of a tomboy. "If you weren't going to have sex with Jake, would you have with Brandon?"

"What does that have to do with anything?"

"You might as well not bother with him either if you aren't planning on having sex. I can tell you this, Crissy girl has had sex with him, and if he can get it from her, why should he bother with you?"

"He's not like that," I insisted with a slight hesitation in my voice. Maybe he was. What did I know? It's not like we ever talked about sex. Had Tyler had sex with Melissa?

"Are you ready to lose your virginity?" she asked.

"What makes you think I'm a virgin?"

"Oh please, you've got it written all over your face," she huffed. This really confused me. I couldn't tell if she was being helpful or just plain mean.

"What do you care about my sex life?" I tried to act like she wasn't getting to me.

"Hon, you asked me, remember?"

"No, I didn't!"

"Look, I don't want you to fool yourself. We girls have to look out for number one." I didn't quite know what Lex was hinting at. "Guys don't fret over girls half as much as girls fret over guys." And as we walked downstairs, I wondered if Lex might be a lesbian. I shooed it away. I wasn't ready to deal with that.

Chapter Eighteen

I waited at Lex's jitney stop for over ten minutes before remembering it was Sunday. The jitney's don't run as often on Sunday and who knew how long it'd be before one would come by. It was a cool, misty morning and the air felt terrific on my face, refreshing and cleansing after my completely creepy night with Jake. My head was in a bit of a fog, too. Lack of sleep, maybe? The effects of alcohol? Who knew why?

I gave up on the jitney and decided to walk home. The island was small enough and it wouldn't take more than forty minutes, I figured. Still faster than the jitney.

My mind wouldn't stop replaying the scenes from Jake's house. What a complete fool I was to walk right into his trap. I mean, it was so obvious. From now on, I would be in control. Jake was a self-obsessed jerk, and that was a fact. Nothing could make me ever like him again. Brandon had made it quite clear that I was out of the picture and that he was back with Crissy. The thought of them kissing, of him holding her, of him gazing into her eyes ... ugh! It all made me want to vomit and rip her head off. He had to "move on" with his life, whatever that meant. I was too much of a reminder of Tyler. Duh. I'm his twin. No one would ever forget him as long as I was around.

But really, what it all came down to was I needed to move on with my life too. I needed to make a change — just for me.

At the house, Mom was fixing up turkey sandwiches for lunch.

"How was the slumber party?" she asked as we sat down to eat.

"Great. Lex and I had a good time doing girly stuff. We painted our nails, watched a movie, gave each other makeovers, you know."

Mom raised her eyebrows and I knew what she was thinking. I was totally B.S.-ing my way through this.

"What? She can be a bit of a girly-girl when she wants to." I hoped the conversation stayed focused on Lex, and that I wouldn't be accidentally tempted into discussing the earlier, more horrible portion of the night.

"I almost forgot: Brandon called for you last night."

"Oh?"

"Sounded like he'd been looking for you for a while."

I muttered a humpf, which was more than I should have.

"What's wrong, honey? You two haven't seen each other in more than a week."

"Nothing. He's just busy with Crissy."

"Are you a little jealous?" Mom teased.

I could feel myself blush, and the red in my cheeks was equal part rage at Brandon and that Mom had totally called me out. I shoveled a big scoop of coleslaw into my mouth. "I don't want to go into it," I said with my mouth full.

"Okay, but you two are really good friends. You should remember that. Don't let anything ruin that."

I rolled my eyes and she just shook her head as she carried her empty plate into the kitchen.

Not an hour later, I got a text from Brandon.

Been trying to find you. Hang out this weekend?

Call me, please?

I buried a scream into my pillow before I wrote back.

Sorry I missed you yesterday. Lex and I went to a party at Jake's house – Jake's this super-hot counselor from camp who has an intense crush on me. Jake and I really hit it off and spent the whole night together.

I cringed as I typed the words.

It was such a killer party. Anyway, I'm busy today. And tomorrow. And for the foreseeable future.

I pressed Send before I had a chance to re-read it, then powered off my phone.

* * * *

On Monday, Jake was waiting for me at the playground for afternoon watch. Mrs. Meyers never did get the scheduling sorted out after my fight with Sherry, and Jake ended up as the permanent replacement. I just couldn't win. Me and playground duty were doomed.

"Hey there," Jake smiled, reaching out to pull me closer to him. I smacked his hand away.

"Ow, what's with the attitude?"

"Leave me alone," I said, turning to look for Sophie, my six-year-old savior. "Hey Sophie, want me to go down the slide with you?"

I followed her cries of "Yes! Yes! Yes!" and left Jake standing alone at the fence. He didn't try to talk to me for the rest of watch, but then, after it was over and all the kids were back inside and onto their next activity, Jake grabbed me again.

"Seriously, I want to make things up to you," he said, looking intently into my eyes. "I'm having another party this weekend," then he moved so that his mouth hovered over my ear. "You'll be there, right? We have unfinished business."

"No," I said pushing him away. "No, Jake, I'm not going to be there."

"But you're my Kit with the gorgeous green eyes." He moved closer and rubbed my arm. When he flashed his killer smile that used to melt my heart, I felt nothing but disgust.

"I'm no one's Kit! And I'm late for gymnastics."

"Fine, you'll miss out on something great," he said, gesturing down his body with his hands.

"I've seen more than enough of that." I shook my head and ran down the hall.

* * * *

On my way home from camp, I detoured to the hair salon next to Weiss's Corner Store. Mom had been going to Chez Paris — which the owner pronounced as Paree — for years, but since my hair was long, straight, and un-styled, I'd never needed to go. Mom could use a ruler and a pair of scissors and usually clean me up pretty decent.

"Hi," I called as I entered the salon.

"Hey, gorgeous, where's your mom?" Candy, Mom's stylist, called from her station where she sat in her chair sipping a coffee and flipping through a *People* magazine, the official salon publication.

"I'm flying solo today," I said.

"Me, too!" Candy exclaimed, always a beacon of optimistic energy. I wondered if she'd been a cheerleader in high school. "Slow afternoon. It'll get busy in another hour. What brings you in?"

I chopped at my hair with mock scissor fingers.

"No!" Candy screamed. "You're *finally* here for a real haircut?!" She set down her mug and magazine enthusiastically.

"Yup! Chop it off and make me pretty."

"I hate to break it to you, Kit, but you're already pretty. In fact, if I do say so myself, girl, you're growing up super

171

fine. You're a heartbreaker in disguise. You just don't know it yet."

I beamed at Candy. "Then it's time to tell the world," I said.

"All right, Miss Thing. Get that booty in my chair, and we'll get you gorgeous."

I flashed my most confident smile at her as I sat tall in the salon chair.

"So, what are you thinking?" she asked as she draped me in a plastic smock.

"I don't even know. Can you just give me a whole new look?"

"You got it, kid."

I couldn't watch as she took the sheers to my long hair. My eyes closed as I imaged a magical transition from tomboy to sex goddess. I was ready to be someone else.

"Okay, open your eyes," Candy instructed. I was stunned at my reflection. "It's a page boy," she smiled as she smacked her gum.

"I look like that girl from *Pulp Fiction!*"

"Yeah, it has that retro look. It screams young and fun or cool and sophisticated. It's perfect for you."

"*So* perfect!" I squealed, tugging at the hair that just breezed past my shoulders. No more split ends. And now I had bangs? Who knew I'd rock bangs? "Is that really *me*?!"

Suddenly, I was nervous about what I'd done. "How do I get it to look like this on my own?"

"You just use your mom's curling iron and curl under the bottom, then spritz a bit of hairspray. Otherwise, it's low maintenance."

I tried to pull it back into a ponytail but it wasn't long enough to gather anymore.

"Nope, your ponytail days are over," Candy smiled, smacking her gum. "Sexy and ponytails don't go together."

I choked back a few tears. The change was so dramatic, overwhelming — so completely wonderful.

I paid Candy with my recently cashed paycheck and rode my bike home, flipping my light new locks in the wind as I raced through the familiar streets. At home, there was a reminder voicemail from the principal's office at ACHS that I had to take my freshman year finals in a few weeks. I'd completely forgotten about them. I didn't even know where my textbooks were. I'd have to dig them out and start studying if I had a prayer of finishing ninth grade.

I'd hoped for a return text from Brandon, but there was nothing. I opened iTunes and found the *Pulp Fiction* soundtrack. I put on some lipstick as my hips swayed to the music.

I was ready to resume my usual routine of listening to the jukebox on the chaise lounge in the backyard when I resolved that my moping and mourning was going to end. My life did not revolve around Brandon, and certainly not around Jake.

I dialed Lex's number.

"Hey, it's Kit."

"Caller ID. I know."

"Right. Can you go out tonight?"

"Sure."

"Fun-N-Stuff sound good?"

"Totally."

"I'll be over to get you in a few."

I left Mom a note and pranced out the door feeling utterly fabulous.

✳ ✳ ✳ ✳

"Geez! I almost didn't recognize you!" Lex exclaimed as she boarded the jitney.

"Check out the new and improved Kit Carlin!" I cried.

"I like it. It's very ... you."

I smiled.

We were on the last hole of miniature golf when I heard someone call my name. I looked across the course and saw Dylan Ryerson from track putting at the ninth hole.

I waved back as he walked toward us. We had just finished our game and Lex took my club a bit roughly before walking to the ticket window to return them. Miss Anti-Social never failed to mope.

"How's it going?" I asked when he was close enough that I would no longer need to scream across the course.

"Good," he smiled brightly. "You cut your hair," he said, sliding his long dark-blonde bangs out of his eyes with his fingers. "I almost didn't recognize you."

"Yeah, I actually just got it cut it today."

Dylan leaned his lanky body against the Lighthouse that marked the eighteenth hole. He was so tall I actually had to tilt my head upwards to talk to him, but his bangs formed a shield over his eyebrows, so from my vantage below, I could see his big brown puppy eyes.

"How's your summer?" I asked the typically appropriate question. Dylan was one of the hundreds of people I hadn't seen since Tyler died.

"It's good. I'm working at Fralinger's. Want any free saltwater taffy? I have tons."

"I bet," I smiled back while looking for Lex. She was sitting, arms crossed and slouched on a bench adjacent to the ticket office. She could wait. It was good practice catching up with someone before school started. Dylan was one of the nicest guys on the track team, always offering up tips to increase speed, jump hurdles, whatever. He was an all-star dynamo on the field.

On instinct, I nervously went to pull my hair behind my ear, forgetting that my ponytail was in the trash at Chez Paris.

"You're at the JCC, aren't you?"

"Yeah," I said a bit surprised he'd remembered such a thing.

"You were really excited when you got the job last spring."

"Good memory."

Dylan smiled as his head dropped and turned to the side. When he surfaced, again I could see that his cheeks were red.

"You here with a girlfriend?" I asked.

"No, I don't have a girlfriend. I'm here with Mike Hetler from track. You? You got a boyfriend?"

"No. I'm here with my friend Lex," I said, pointing in her direction. "We work together at the JCC."

Dylan nodded and shuffled his feet.

"Are you going to Brandon's birthday party?" Dylan asked.

I would like to think that I hadn't remembered it, that I was surprised at the mention of it, but of course I'd been agonizing over whether or not to go. I'd never missed Brandon's birthday. Ever.

"Haven't decided," I answered.

"I just assumed, because of Tyler, that you two were ..."

"Were what?" I asked nervously, cutting him off.

"Well, friends. You three used to hang out a lot. It must be really hard. I ... I, well, I just don't know what to ..."

"It's okay. You don't have to say anything," I jumped in, saving him from additional, unnecessary awkwardness.

"What I wanted to say was — or I mean ask, was — do you want to go to the party with me?"

"A date?" I questioned in a way that came across unnecessarily snotty. Really, I was just in shock.

"You know, if you want . . . you don't have to."

"Sorry! No, that would be great, Dylan. Let's do it."

"Really?" His dark brown eyes brightened.

"Yup."

"God, I should have done this a lot sooner."

I raised my eyebrows.

"Asked you out. I'd been wanting to all through track season. I just couldn't quite get around to it. Then Tyler ... well, then you were gone."

"I'm glad you did."

Dylan beamed as he plugged my phone number into his phone.

✳ ✳ ✳ ✳

"Who was that?" Lex asked as we met at the exit.

"Dylan, a guy from the track team."

"He seemed really into you."

"He asked me to go to Brandon's birthday party with him."

"You said no I hope."

"I said I'd go."

"Oh, Kit."

"Let's go get slushies!" I suggested in a childlike tone. Why couldn't she be my friend for once and not my conscience?

"So, how do you deal so well?" I asked as we approached our favorite slushy stand.

"Deal with what?"

"Losing your parents? Moving away from where you grew up, all of it?"

"I don't know. I just do."

"My parents are fighting like crazy all the time or just not talking. I don't know if they're going to make it," I said. Lex didn't respond.

We got our slushies and leaned against the rail of the boardwalk, listening to the voices of the crowd mix with the crashing waves.

"It's crap like this that makes us stronger," Lex explained. "You're tough, you'll survive."

I realized in that moment, as Lex sat on the rail of the boardwalk slurping her slushy, that one of the main reasons I liked hanging around with her was that when we were together I was no longer the tomboy. She made me look and feel feminine. None of the other girls I knew — Melissa, Crissy, my old friends at Holy Spirit, even Sherry — could do that. They were all trying to out-do each other for the closest resemblance to a *Vogue* magazine cover girl. Lex didn't take anything from anyone, and I'm quite sure she had never attempted mascara. There wasn't a fake bone in her body and if you ever thought of crossing her, those wolf eyes would voodoo you to the wall.

"You never told me how your parents died."

"They got hit by a drunk driver."

"Oh."

"That picture you were looking at on my dresser. That was taken the night they were killed. They were out to dinner for their anniversary."

"Wow."

Lex nodded.

"Were they happy to be married? Did they love each other?"

"Yeah, I think so."

"That's good. My dad hardly comes home before bedtime. He's always at the shop or out with sailing buddies."

"Or at a motel with a hooker."

"Lex!"

"Well, this is Atlantic City," she said as she jumped off the rail and shot her empty cup like a basketball into the trashcan, then reached for mine to do the same. I handed it to her, still unsure whether our conversation had ended. "They're practically on every street corner."

"That's disgusting."

"Maybe not to your dad."

"Okay, thanks for the gross visual. Now I need to wash my brain out with soap."

I slug punched Lex and we laughed all the way to the jitney stop.

When I got home, the porch light was on and I could see Dad watching TV in the living room. He had a beer in his hand. I prayed that he was drunk and wouldn't know what time it was.

"Hi, Dad," I called as I walked in the front door.

"How was your night?" he asked, his eyes never leaving the TV.

"Fine. Lex and I had a great time."

"That's good," he called. Whew, I was home free.

"Well, I'm tired, better go to bed," I said, starting up the stairs.

"Eh, just a minute. Aren't you forgetting something?"

"Hmm?" I asked, as cute and innocently as I could.

"Your curfew. You still have one and you were supposed to be home forty minutes ago," he said, eyeing the living room clock.

"I'm sorry," I said. "I know; Lex and I missed the 11 o'clock bus. I'm not sure which one we ended up catching."

"Next time, call," he ordered, and went back to watching TV.

"Right, next time I'll call. Sorry," I apologized. As I walked upstairs, it occurred to me that he didn't notice my haircut. With Dad still awake, Tyler's journal would have to wait for another night. I did a little dance on the way to my bedroom, running my fingers through my new short hair and thinking about Dylan.

Chapter Nineteen

Monday's mail brought a package from Grandma. It made me think how cool it would be, to live in an age when people still wrote letters. The only thing I consistently got in the mail were appointment reminders from doctors and dentists.

August 2nd

Dear Kit,

I'm so glad you are enjoying the books. Here is one about a psychologist who regresses people so that they can learn about their past lives. I've also thrown in a fun little astrology book.

I was delighted to read that you've made a new friend at camp and yes, since you are a Gemini, you would get along well with her being an Aquarius. You're both air signs (which may mean you both think too much)!

I was saddened to hear of your fight. No matter how tough life gets, Kit, please don't turn to violence as a way to solve things. I know your heart is good and I wouldn't want to see it corrupted by the evil forces that fall prey on weakness. Be strong but be positive.

Life for me is going fine. I'm back into the swing of things and hitting the shuffleboard circuit hard. I go to the beach nearly every day and walk a good four miles. I just finished reading my fifth novel this month! Retired life ain't too bad.

I think about Tyler and pray for him often, and I hope his absence is getting easier on you. I'm so happy to hear about the wonderful friends you have in your life. Write again soon! It was such a delight to receive your letter.

Love you,
Grandma

I set the letter down and immediately looked up Leo in the astrology book — Brandon's sign. Leo's have a flair for drama and a noble presence. They love attention, but can be very supportive and generous as well. They have a magnetic personality. I slammed the book shut. When was Dylan's birthday? I'd have to ask him.

✳ ✳ ✳ ✳

Thursday was the day I'd been dreading all week: Cousin Ari's homecoming dinner. He'd just returned last weekend from his summer in Israel and it was time for a family get-together. Ari and I were never close, and I dreaded a night of being locked in the house with him, Aunt Deborah, and Uncle David. Mom said that Ari wanted to invite his new girlfriend, Rachel, someone who was with him on the Israel trip, but she couldn't make it to dinner. I couldn't imagine what someone would look like who would date Ari, and half-wished she was coming just so I could see.

"Hello." I faked a smile as I greeted them at the door.

"Hello, Kit," Aunt Deborah said as Uncle David nodded hello. "Hey" was all I got from Ari, as if I'd just seen him yesterday.

"You look lovely tonight, Kit. Are you wearing makeup?" Aunt Deborah asked.

"No, I never wear makeup."

"I didn't think so. You must just be tan. You don't look washed out like the last time I saw you."

Aunt Deborah was getting her digs in, right out of the gate. It was going to be a long night,

"Oh, I know!" she exclaimed. "You cut your hair!"

I nodded.

"It's cute," she said. I couldn't tell if that was meant to be condescending or sincere, but I didn't really care.

"Hello, hello!" Mom sang as she came into the foyer. She was wearing a fuchsia sundress that clashed horribly with her red-and-white-striped apron. "Help yourselves to appetizers in the living room. I have to finish up a few things," she said before dancing her way back to the kitchen.

"We would have made it sooner if it hadn't been for that damn yacht," Uncle David called after Mom, over-exaggerating as usual. The couch buckled from his weight. Then, in one smooth motion, he leaned forward, grabbed a chip, and began scooping up spinach dip like the chip was his own personal food shovel. He leaned back onto the couch and talked while he chewed with his mouth open. Like a mini-me – although not so mini — Ari followed suit, kicking up his feet, shoes and all, onto the coffee table, right next to the food. Was I honestly related to these people?

Aunt Deborah's body language told me we were in for one of those stories where she and Uncle David shared lines back and forth. I hated when they did that.

181

"Oh, some big fancy-schmancy yacht had the drawbridge up on the other side of the causeway from Jerome Avenue," Aunt Deborah continued. Even though the kitchen wasn't more than ten feet from the living room, they were both talking as loudly as they could to make sure that Mom could hear. Maybe they were trying to ensure that the neighbors could hear, too.

"But then it holds up traffic for at least two miles and it's a nightmare," Uncle David shouted, spraying food as he yelled.

"Did you hear about the Weinstein's new boat?" Aunt Deborah called to Mom. "Such extravagance," she continued. "Do they need the whole world to know how wealthy they are? You heard that Barbara inherited all that money?"

She droned on and on about some family I didn't know, eventually leaving the living room to join Mom in the kitchen. I remained like an owl, perched on my favorite chair on the other side of the room, watching this invasion that had taken over my house.

Ari still hadn't said a word or stopped eating. He must have gained forty pounds in Israel. His body was covered in new rolls of fat. I think I saw him pick his nose before he reached for a deviled egg.

"So, Kit," Aunt Deborah yelled from the kitchen. "I'm running the Miss America planning committee again."

I froze. I knew where she was going. "You mean for the parade?" I clarified. Aunt Deborah had a way of making her role in matters sound much grander than they actually were.

The night before the Miss America contest, there was always a parade on the boardwalk and each state got its own float. She was on the committee for the parade, not the pageant.

"Yes, yes," she shooed my words away as she returned to the living room, as though the details didn't matter. "This year, the Atlantic City float is being sponsored by Harrah's

Casino. Their theme is Summertime at the Beach. They need a few teenagers to ride the float and look like they're playing at the beach, you know, with Frisbees and those sorts of things. I thought it was a marvelous idea, so I signed you all up."

"Who's all of us?" I pressed, nervous that her idea of everyone was what I feared most.

"You, Ari, and Rachel, of course." Of course.

"Oh, great," I sighed, immediately brainstorming excuses that were believable enough to get me out of it.

"Oh, don't act all melodramatic. You and Rachel will look adorable." Adorable, exactly the look I was striving for.

"The last time I did this for you, I froze my butt off all night," I reminded her.

"Kit!" Mom scolded from the kitchen.

"Only you would look a gift horse in the mouth. If you were my child ..." Aunt Deborah started, but Uncle David shook his head like I was a lost cause and she stopped. "Aren't you all so excited to hear about Ari's trip?" she asked, changing the subject, but also glaring at Uncle David for cutting her off.

"You did bring the flash drive, Ari, didn't you?" Mom called.

"Yeah, I've got an hour and a half of footage and over six hundred photos."

No! Someone come rescue me, please!

"Susan, where the devil is Jeff?" Uncle David called into the kitchen.

"What was that?"

"He's down at the marina," I answered for Mom. "He should be here any minute." But I didn't believe it. An hour ago, I overheard Mom on the phone with Dad and the call wasn't going well. She'd said, "Don't tell me you forgot, Jeff. Why? I want to know why." The expression on her face was pained. "Can you at least get here by the time dinner's served? You know, I don't ask much of you anymore around here." When she hung up, her eyes were moist and she began furiously dicing the carrots. I was scared she'd cut off a finger.

"How is your job at the JCC going?" Aunt Deborah asked.

"Fine."

"I get good reports. Mrs. Meyers always has such kind things to say about you."

I laughed to myself. Did nobody tell Aunt Deborah about me getting suspended? I wouldn't be surprised. She was so powerful at the JCC that I doubt anybody would dare say anything negative to her, especially since she was in charge of fundraising. Now that I thought of it, maybe that was why I was let back to camp after all, and not because of Louise's letter.

Mom forgot to make rice to accompany the stir-fry so dinner was delayed an extra half-hour. This made Uncle David frustrated so he single-handedly finished off the spinach dip. It did allow time for Dad to get home, though, and I tried to figure out if Mom forgot the rice on purpose.

"Sorry I'm late, everyone. Busy time of year. Go ahead and start eating and I'll join in a minute. Just need to clean up and get out of these grubs," Dad called from the foyer. We were all at the table and had begun passing dishes. He joined us about fifteen minutes into the meal, taking the open seat next to me.

Ari remained quiet through dinner and it was weird — nobody mentioned Tyler the whole night — well, not directly anyway. The dinner talk revolved around what was new with the JCC board, gossipy things mostly, and Uncle David's latest business venture.

Uncle David was a venture capitalist, which I'd learned was a fancy term for someone who gave techie geeks money and hoped they'd make him even more money with their inventions. Apparently, he knew how to sniff out a good geek because he was always making more and more money.

Dad barely said a word, but he pretended to be interested in what Uncle David was saying. Uncle David never asked about Dad's boat shop, and Dad never mentioned it.

When Uncle David made a comment about Dad's hair, it quieted the whole table. Dad had gone from black to grey in the span of the summer, but only someone like Uncle David would actually say something. To Uncle David, Dad was a loser. He couldn't provide the same material things for his family that Uncle David did for his. I actually overheard him say that to Mom once.

"So, Linda tells me you're dropping the case," Aunt Deborah tossed out toward the end of dinner.

"Really?" I asked. This was the first I'd heard of it.

"Yes," Dad answered for her. "There never was a case."

"Jeff!"

"What, Susan? It's true. You just needed Linda to go through the motions to prove that to you."

I watched the volley between Mom and Dad and cringed.

"Yes, Linda said they ran it by a test jury and it flopped," Aunt Deborah added, not that Mom needed the extra stinger. I didn't even realize it had gotten to a test jury, but then again, I'd worked pretty hard to avoid any discussions concerning the case.

"That's pretty much what happened," Mom agreed.

"We just need to move on," Dad smiled tightly, and then stabbed another chicken chunk with his fork.

I looked at Mom, but she wasn't making eye contact with anyone.

After dinner, Mom, Aunt Deborah, and I cleared the table while the guys relaxed in the living room, although I doubt it was very relaxing for Dad. After the dishes were done, we joined them. It never made sense to me why women always had to slave in the kitchen. It was enough to make me never want to get married. Mom put on a pot of decaf coffee for Ari's slideshow. I begged her to let me have a cup and she said I could. The trick to getting her to say yes was knowing when she lacked the energy to fight any more battles for the day.

"They don't have a projection screen?" Ari whined to Uncle David, as I walked in holding a tray of coffee mugs, a pitcher of cream and a dish of sugar. Dad looked about a minute away from passing out on his recliner.

"This laptop will be fine," Uncle David assured him.

"The pictures won't look right." Ari continued whining, but Uncle David shrugged his shoulders at Ari as if to say they were stuck with our horrible lame-ass technology set-up. I wanted to suggest we skip the show altogether, and that they could go home, but I didn't. At least Dad would have been in my court on that one.

The videos dragged on and on. Ari was a horrible photographer. Almost every video had people's heads chopped off. He tried to blame it on having to show the movie on his computer instead of a home theater. I doubted that was the issue.

His new girlfriend was *all* over the place. There's Rachel in front of the Wailing Wall! There's Rachel on top of Masada! There's Rachel in her bikini on a beach in Tel Aviv! There's Rachel buying a pastry! Oy vey! Rachel was ultra skinny and had super short, boring brown hair that was covered by a bandana in almost every shot. Her features were abnormally tiny, making her seem like a little girl. I looked at Ari's plump body and wondered how far they'd gone, but only for a second.

"The first week I spent with Grandma and Grandpa Steinberg who live in Jerusalem," Ari explained. "They invited me to spend the whole summer with them next year."

"Yes, honey, we'll definitely arrange that," Aunt Deborah assured him. "In fact, maybe Kit would like to go, too. She never got a chance to know her grandparents ..."

Dad cut her off. "Kit's not going to the Middle East." I thanked Dad with my eyes, and he winked back. Besides discussions about the case, I couldn't remember the last time Dad and I were on the same page.

"I'm going to Florida next summer," I told them. "And I'm staying with Grandma Carlin."

"Nobody goes to Florida in the summer, sweetie," Aunt Deborah grinned.

"Let's see the rest of the show," Mom directed Ari. I shifted uncomfortably in my chair. I was most certainly not going to Israel next summer, and I was most certainly never spending a summer with Ari.

"After spending time in Jerusalem, I met up with my Hebrew Academy friends and we began our tour of the country. The last few weeks, we stayed on a Kibbutz. Do you know what a Kibbutz is, Kit?"

"Yes," I sighed. Just because The Boy Wonder went to Hebrew school didn't mean I was dumb about everything Jewish. "And I know that you have to work when you stay at a Kibbutz. What did you do?" I asked. Ari had never worked a day in his life. He probably wouldn't even know how to turn on a vacuum, much less muck out a pig stall.

"We would help harvest the grapes and clean them. We were even allowed some wine," Ari beamed while Aunt Deborah sighed.

Ari continued with the videos for another half-hour before we moved onto the print photos. At ten o'clock, I feigned a stomachache so I could be excused. I went to my room and read one of Brandon's *Rolling Stones* that I'd borrowed before he'd lost most of them in the storm. I checked my phone. Still nothing. Once I heard Mom and Dad close the door to their bedroom, I snuck into Tyler's room.

August 6th

Tyler,

Well, you got lucky and missed the most horrible night ever! Ari was showing off his poor photography and video skills and his new girlfriend, Rachel. I don't remember him ever having a girlfriend, do you?

Aunt Deborah mentioned something about me going to Israel with him next summer. NO WAY! I told everyone that I am going to Florida, which I still plan to do.

Dad and I were getting along better than we have all summer. I keep avoiding talking to you about Mom and Dad because it's too painful to think about. They aren't in a good place. Dad keeps disappearing for longer and longer amounts of time and, well, I think there's a good chance divorce is on the horizon. I hate to even write the word, like I might make it come true, but you know, I don't even know if I'm against it anymore. There's always so much tension between them and when Dad's here, the house feels suffocating. He makes it so clear he doesn't want to be here. Like this isn't his real home anymore.

I wish I could go off to college now and just come visit for summers and school breaks. I still

188

have three years to go though, so guess I'd better come up with some heavy-duty coping mechanisms beyond Grandma's yoga breathing. On that note, I should really go to bed. Sleep is my favorite coping mechanism at the moment.

Good night and pleasant dreams!

K

Chapter Twenty

Dad was home on time for dinner, so I knew something was up. Mom looked all fakey cheerful as she brought the casserole dish to the dining room table and smoothed out her apron in total OCD fashion. It all seemed too good to be true, too perfect, so I played along.

"Need a hand?" I asked.

"I've got it, hon," Mom brushed off my question with a wave of her hand before walking quickly back into the kitchen. "Don't you need to get ready for the party?" she called behind her.

It was 5 o'clock and Dylan wouldn't be coming for another three hours to pick me up for Brandon's party. Brandon's party. I still got a thrill imagining the look on Brandon's face when he saw me with Dylan.

"I'm pretty much ready," I called to her. "Just need to 'put on my blush' before Dylan comes over," I smiled, following her into the kitchen and pinching my cheeks to elicit a grin from Mom. When I was young and wanted makeup, she'd pinch my cheeks to make them turn red. "There!" she exclaim. "Now you're wearing blush!"

It was getting a little easier to make her smile, but it still took a lot of work. I wondered when or if the day would ever come where the simple things would be easy again, when I wouldn't have to try at all, when a smile would just happen.

"You sound so grown up," she sighed and stopped a minute to look at me.

I smiled a thank you then grabbed a clean glass from the dish drain and filled it up with water.

"So, what's with the nice dishes and Dad being home for dinner?"

"Nothing." Mom's voice was shaky. Not good. I stared at her, demanding more information, but she ignored me and turned her attention back to the food prep.

That ended my five minutes of me-time from Mom, so I headed up to my room and decided to await whatever fate was coming with dinner. I brushed and re-brushed my flip, spraying more hairspray than necessary to keep the 'do in place. Mom was so excited I had a date that she'd let me borrow her makeup. No more fake blush. Rather than choosing between my two lipsticks, I now had fifteen of them. Coral Sand, Mauve Mayhem, Sparkling Sunrise — the choices in color were as overwhelming as the names were silly. I cued up *Light My Fire* by The Doors and put it on Repeat. I sang the lyrics into my hairbrush while I flipped my hair back and forth, waiting for dinner, for Dylan, for the night to start already.

Mom called up the stairs around 5:30. Dad was already sitting at the table when I walked into the dining room. Everyone was quiet. The table looked strange, with Dad occupying his normal seat. I'd gotten used to it being just Mom and me all summer. I took my usual seat and the empty spot where Tyler would have been seemed bigger than ever, like this big hole that could just suck us all in. I looked away from the empty chair and reached for the casserole dish, scooping out a large chunk of cheesy, noodley goodness. Mom and Dad watched me with their hands in their laps.

"Okay, you two. You're freaking me out. What's going on?"

"Well," Mom started, but then turned her head away. I could tell she was crying.

"It's not working out," Dad said, moving his elbows onto the table and shaking his head. He wouldn't look at Mom. "I'm sorry Kit. I'm really, really sorry."

There was no way I was going to eat the casserole I just scooped onto my plate.

"I'm moving out," Dad finished.

The words pummeled me. "Is this for real?" I asked Mom. She was full-on crying and her sobs triggered my own tears. I could only imagine the black rivulets of mascara dripping down my face.

"Yes," she squeaked out, but she was staring out the window. I'd never felt so alone in the company of my family.

"When?" I asked Dad as I reached for Mom's hand. She was shaking.

"Tomorrow," Dad replied, all calm and collected. I wanted to take Mom and run away from him, from this house, from all of its terrible memories!

"Seriously? You can't stand us for one more day?" I snapped and suddenly my tears were replaced with rage.

"It's just a separation. I need some time to sort things out. We all do."

"What's to sort out? I'm your daughter. She's your wife." I pointed at Mom as I let go of her hand and pushed my chair away hard, sending it crashing to the floor. "We're the most important people to you. I'm sorry if your precious son is gone, but we need you too."

"Don't bring Tyler into this."

"It's all about Tyler. It's always about him! Are you crazy?! We're nothing to you since he died!"

"Kit," Mom started, but I couldn't hear any more blah blah bullshit. Dad wouldn't look at me.

"Mom and I will be fine! We don't need you!" I yelled. "Mom can find someone better!"

"Kit!" Mom cried out, pleading with her eyes for me to stop. I wouldn't. Someone had to stand up for Mom, for us.

192

"In fact, maybe Mom will find someone and start a new family, and then we won't even need you anymore! I bet you'd love that!"

Now Dad pushed himself away, slammed his chair into the table, and stormed off toward the garage.

"Jeff, please, we need to talk through this together," Mom begged him to stay, extending her arm as he walked by, but he brushed her off. We heard the garage door slam behind him.

"We're going to be okay," I said, rubbing Mom's shoulders and glaring in the direction of the garage. "I have lots of friends who have divorced parents."

"We're not getting divorced, just separating." Mom wiped her tears with her apron.

"Okay, separated. But if it ends in divorce, it will be okay too. I just may never speak to Dad again."

"Your father loves you very much."

"Yeah, well, maybe someday he'll learn to show it. For now, fuck him."

"Excuse me?!"

"It's time for us all to grow up, Mom. I have a party to get ready for. Are you going to be okay?"

"I'm fine," Mom said, "I don't want to ruin your big night."

I coughed back a scream. For not wanting to ruin my night, she certainly wasn't trying very hard.

"Don't you want any casserole before you go? It's your favorite, tuna with crispy cornflake crust." She managed a smile through her tears, telling me she was going to be okay.

"I'll have it for lunch tomorrow. I can't eat now." I left Mom and went to my room to redo my makeup, but first to cry in peace.

When I heard Dylan's dad's car pull into our driveway, I raced to pick a lipstick, ending up with Coral Sand. After carefully applying it, I stuck the lipstick in my purse for touchups later. Peeking out the window before heading downstairs, I saw Dylan carrying a yellow rose. Where had this guy been all my life? Right in front of my eyes, apparently, and I was too caught up in Brandon to notice.

I tried my best to push Dad and Mom and tonight's drama to the back of my mind. From this moment on, the night needed to be all about me. Not Tyler. Not my parents. Me. In a way, it was my coming-out party, like in the South how they have those debutante balls, some kind of legacy from the 1800s. It would be the first time my friends from school, and more importantly, Brandon, would see the new and improved Kit — the confident, sexy, new Kit.

Admiring myself in the mirror, I did a last-minute check before leaving my room. I'd decided on the same outfit that I'd worn to Jake's party, hoping this time it would bring me better luck. It had to. The shimmery tank top looked fantastic with the lipstick, and I loved how the edges of my hair brushed my naked shoulders. Finally, I'd found a style that pulled attention away from my flat chest.

"Hi," I smiled and waved as I walked down the stairs. Dylan was standing in the foyer awkwardly holding a rose. Mom was glowing as much as she was capable of these days, although her eyes were still a watery red. Dad hadn't come back inside and I wondered when I'd see him again. Where was he moving? Would he get joint custody, so that I'd have to spend some weekends and holidays with him? No, tonight was just for me. All of that could wait.

"You look amazing," Dylan said, barely able to get out the words as he handed me the flower. I looked into his eyes, wishing that I'd swoon the way I once did with Jake and always did with Brandon, but perhaps that butterfly sensation was just a trail to heartbreak. This was the kind of thing that would last — the reason girls had boyfriends for years: strong, steady, caring relationships. I could tell Dylan was true boyfriend material.

"Thanks," I blushed, taking the rose, but not really knowing what to do with it.

"Let me go put that in some water," Mom said, "and I'll take it up to your room."

"My dad's outside," Dylan said, shuffling his feet in his sport sandals. He was wearing the summer uniform of every guy from our high school: baggy shorts that hung low below the belt line, Phillies T-shirt, and coral surfer necklace tight around his neck.

"Okay, you kids, have a good night. And Kit, I need you home by midnight," Mom smiled as she left us and walked into the kitchen.

✳ ✳ ✳ ✳

When we pulled up to Brandon's house, my stomach filled with a swarm of butterflies. How could I just stroll into that house like nothing had happened? We said goodbye to Dylan's dad and walked up to the house. Dylan knocked on Brandon's front door while I, a good step behind him, started taking deep breaths. I'd never knocked on Brandon's door before. I always went right in.

"Kit, is that you?" Mrs. Garner smiled as she opened the door wide.

I beamed. The transformation worked!

"Oh, yeah," I blushed, tucking a lock of hair behind my ear.

"Well, I'll be! If you aren't the cat's meow! Let me see you!" She played with my hair and made me twirl around. Dylan smiled like I was an accessory of his, a glittering bracelet he could show off on his arm. "Wait until Brandon sees you," she said.

I coughed and Dylan grabbed hold of my hand.

"Mrs. Garner, this is my date, Dylan Ryerson. He's on the track team with Brandon and me."

"Nice to meet you, Dylan. You kids come in."

Dylan placed his hand on my lower back, guiding me up the stairs and into the living room. It felt both warm and comforting, like he was there to catch me if I fell, which felt like a real possibility. There were kids on the couch, others hovering around a table of food in the dining room, crowds standing in the kitchen. I hadn't seen any of these people since I'd left school at the start of summer. They were a memory minefield as many had a Tyler story attached to them. After all, this was Tyler's best friend's birthday party, and most of these people were Tyler's friends, too.

It seemed as if people were staring and whispering as I went by. I'd become that untouchable, the girl with a dark cloud over her. I thought I even heard a "There she is" as I walked past some cheerleaders. Melissa waved to me from the other side of the room, but didn't make the effort to come over and say hi, which was fine by me. I had no interest in being forced to talk to her.

As Dylan and I made our way, I searched for Brandon and Crissy. I was desperate to know what she looked like post-Europe, and prayed that I looked better.

"Hey, Tomquake!" Dylan called, slapping a guy I vaguely knew on the back.

"Hey, Big D!" Tomquake cheered. I missed Lex.

After forgetting that I was there, Dylan introduced me to "Tomquake." I wanted to ask where he got the nickname, but then we were off and mingling again and it really didn't matter. Mrs. Garner passed by, offering lemonade.

"I haven't seen Brandon or Crissy yet," I told her in my most casual tone, hoping Dylan couldn't hear the tension in my voice.

"Oh, honey, didn't Brandon tell you? He and Crissy broke up."

The lemonade she had just handed me slipped right out of my grasp and landed in a splash on the floor. My body, frozen, couldn't react.

"You okay?" Dylan asked, picking the empty plastic cup up from the floor. My legs and shoes were wet with lemonade.

I nodded that I was okay, but I was far from okay. Brandon and Crissy had broken up? Why? Who initiated? Weren't they great just a few days ago? Since when? Questions coursed through me in rapid-fire succession.

"Don't worry. I'll just go grab a rag," Mrs. Garner rushed to the kitchen.

"What was that about?" Dylan pressed.

"I don't know. I guess I lost my grip," I said, flustered. Dylan eyed me skeptically

"What? It was slippery," I protested, perhaps a bit too strongly.

Mrs. Garner returned and mopped up the lemonade and wiped off my legs.

"Let me get that," I offered. "I'm so sorry."

"Oh, these things happen. Don't you worry about a thing," she offered in her Southern drawl. "Brandon's outside by the pool, dear. Oh, and Crissy's here, too, but I'm not sure where she went. She's probably with Melissa. I'll take care of this. You kids go enjoy the party."

Crissy was here, but they'd broken up? What was going on? What was happening to this world?

Outside, a small group of Tyler and Brandon's friends had formed near the edge of the pool. It was too stormy and overcast for swimming, but a few were in the pool anyway, and the patio echoed with cries of "Marco! Polo!"

Brandon spotted me first. His eyes widened and I finally had the *Grease* moment I'd been praying for. Goodbye, Sandra Dee. The last time Brandon saw me was that afternoon on the beach, when my wet ponytail said: *best friend's sister, girl next door, no one to notice.* That girl was gone.

Brandon started walking toward us, and my heart pounded in rhythm with his steps. Dylan put his arm around my shoulder, twirling his fingers in the flip of my hair in that way boys do when they own someone. Part of me wanted to push him away and run to Brandon. Instead, I snuggled in closer.

"Hi," Brandon said, in the most detached tone imaginable. Hearing such coldness from him was unbearable. How had things ended up so wrong?

"Hi," I returned as nonchalantly as I could muster — but inside I was breaking.

"Hey, Dylan, glad you could make it," Brandon said, but the whole time his eyes were fixed on Dylan's arm around my shoulder.

"Where's Jason?" I asked as a means of distraction.

"Dad took him and Daniel to Chuck E. Cheese."

"Ah, good call."

"Can I offer you guys a drink?" Brandon asked. I wished I could ask for something alcoholic in mine.

"Yeah, Kit dropped her lemonade," Dylan spoke for me. "I'll take a Coke."

"I'll get you a new one." Brandon knew that I absolutely loved his mom's lemonade. His presumed intimacy, though, was unbearable.

"No, I'll take a Coke, too," I said. Brandon stared a moment longer, and I could feel Dylan gripping me tighter. We followed Brandon to the poolside bar, but on the way, Dylan ran into another friend.

"I'll be right there," Dylan called as he stopped to say hi. Brandon and I continued on toward the bar.

"You cut your hair," Brandon said. He wouldn't stop staring. "When did you do that?"

"What happened with Crissy?" I asked, trying to contain the shake in my voice.

"Since when are you seeing Ryerson?" he snapped as he popped a can of Coke. Our fingers brushed when he handed it to me and chills travelled up my spine. I ran a hand through the flip in my hair trying to shake out the sensation.

"What's it to you?"

"Crissy and I broke up last week."

"So I heard."

"Word gets around fast, I guess. She showed up anyway. Never could say no to a party."

"So did she leave you for a Euro-trash man?" I sneered as I followed his lead and sat on an empty stool. I wasn't used to wearing sandals with heels and my feet were killing me.

"I broke up with her."

I gulped my Coke, and forgetting it wasn't lemonade, cringed in pain at the rush of carbonation exploding against the back of my throat. I was not a fan of soda.

"Are you two really an item?" Brandon asked, seriously concerned.

"Yeah," I said, not wanting to confess that it was our first date.

"What happened to Jake?"

"Jake?" I asked, wondering how Brandon knew about him.

"Yeah, the um, hot counselor who was really into you?"

Oh, the text. Shit.

"That's over," I said as nonchalantly as possible.

"Well, you seem to be whipping through them fast these days. Hope Dylan's not on The Heartbreak Express too."

"Screw you." I left my nearly full can of Coke on the bar and went in search of Dylan.

"Hi, Kit!" Crissy and Melissa shrilled in unison as Dylan and I walked back inside. I sighed and walked their way.

"Welcome back," I said to Crissy.

"Thanks! Love the new 'do, Kit," Crissy smiled as she reached out for a hug.

"Thanks," I said, reluctantly hugging her back. "So, how was your summer?"

"Oh, Europe was super great, and OMG, do I have some incredible stories! It was all such just amazing fabulosity, you know?"

"No, I don't," I sighed. "I've never been."

"Oh, well you should really go to Geneva sometime," she started and for the next few minutes, I half-tuned out everything she said as my eyes scanned the room to see if Brandon had come back inside. As she droned on about opera and cafés, I could only think about how I'd spent the whole summer with her boyfriend, praying that he was really in love with me.

"So you heard about Brandon and me?" Crissy asked.

I nodded my head and gulped hard.

"Yeah, well, whatever. Ian Clark has been just dying to go out with me, as has Derek Bacchio. Honestly, it's hard to choose. They're both so hot."

"I'm going to go play video games with Tomquake," Dylan interrupted.

"I'll join you," I said, anxious to get away from Crissy.

"Nice," Crissy nodded her approval at me being with Dylan after he'd turned his back. I smiled at her and followed him away. If she only knew.

Dylan was a fairly attentive date; whenever we were together he always held my hand or left his hand on my back. About an hour later, Dylan was still playing video games, and I excused myself to go to the bathroom. I reapplied my lipstick, feeling proud that I'd not only brought it but then remembered to use it. Instead of going back to Dylan, I found myself heading out to the pool. I needed to get some air. What had happened to my *Grease* moment? This night was a complete disaster.

The deck was empty now, most of the party either in front of the TV playing games or upstairs in the living room. I leaned on the railing overlooking the back bay. Would tonight be the last time I'd set foot in Brandon's house? Nostalgia overtook me as I looked at the pool and remembered so many fun afternoons with Tyler and Brandon. I missed Tyler terribly in that moment, more than I'd let myself in weeks. Dylan was a nice distraction, but when everything peeled away, the grief was still there, heavy on my heart. I wondered if it was the same for Brandon, Melissa, and everyone else who was close to him. Things had changed so much since he left. Would he even recognize any of us if he walked back into this world tonight?

Then I started thinking about Mom and Dad, and the tears began to form.

"Hey, Trouble," I heard Brandon's voice behind me and turned to see him walking my way. "Sorry about earlier. I didn't mean to be a jerk."

"Apology accepted," I said, attempting to swallow my tears.

So, you finally ditched Ryerson for a few minutes."

I smiled, still lost in my memories. "Didn't know you were watching," I said, challenging him. "I was just thinking about last year's party. Remember the island Tyler created in the pool by stringing all the rafts together."

Brandon nodded.

"That was the night Tyler and Melissa hooked up for the first time," I said.

"Yup."

"And soon after that, you and Crissy got back together."

He looked around.

"She's upstairs."

"Why did she have to come?" Brandon asked, more rhetorically than not. He put his head into his hands, then looked at me. "So, how serious is this thing with Dylan, anyway?"

I turned back to look out over the bay. The storm clouds had moved on and the stars were peeking through the wispy clouds that remained, as was the subtle glow of the moon. I couldn't see myself with Dylan at this party next year. I didn't really know if I could see Dylan in my life once school started, which was just a few weeks away. He was nice, but nice only went so far. Try as I might, there were just no sparks.

"Why?"

"It surprised me, I guess."

"That someone could like me?" I snapped. "It's not that shocking you know. Some people may actually find me attractive ..."

"Stop it." Brandon's serious tone caught me off guard. "All right, I'm jealous. When Crissy and I broke up ... well, I guess I just figured ..."

"Figured what?"

"It wasn't right between us anymore. She'd changed after Europe, and I guess I'd changed because of you. Every time I kissed her, I couldn't help but think ...," Brandon shuffled his feet and stared at the deck. My heart was pounding about a million miles a minute, while my head tried to wipe clear the image of them all lip-locked and snuggly. "Nah, forget it."

"You couldn't help but think what?" I pressed. I needed to hear him say it.

"I just wished I was kissing you."

And that was it. The confession was finally released. The truth I'd known had been locked in there all summer was finally out in the open. I lost my voice for a moment. *He picked me. He honestly picked me.* I leaned forward and pressed my lips against his as if I were sealing it with a kiss.

Then I stepped back and caution set in. "Do not mess with me, Brandon." My defensive side was still on guard. I needed it to be for real this time, not out of loneliness and confusion or whatever else he was feeling. "Please do not mess with me," I begged.

Brandon leaned over, grasped my head in his hands, and pulled my face to his. His lips pressed hard against mine. My head wanted to fight, but my heart and my body melted into his. I floated as images of Tyler and Dylan dodged in and out of my mind, telling me it was wrong, cruel, but somehow it wasn't. It was perfect.

"Where's the birthday boy?" Someone asked as the sliding door opened. I pulled free from Brandon's kiss to look over his shoulder. It was his mom holding an enormous sheet cake, glowing with candles. Behind her was the entire party singing "Happy Birthday." I looked back at Brandon and in the moonlight reflection off the water, I could see the Coral Sand lipstick all over his mouth.

"What the fuck!" Crissy screamed over the birthday song. Everyone stopped. Mrs. Garner looked horrified at Crissy's language. I almost started giggling, but choked it back. Mrs. Garner looked back at us, and underneath her shock was a happiness that was clear. For the first time, I wondered what my folks would think.

Neither Brandon nor I spoke, but Brandon reached for my hand and clasped it tight. My breath caught in my throat as I tried to take in the wonderfulness and horror of the moment. "Brandon, you want to explain what's happening here?" Crissy demanded.

"Let's head back inside," Mrs. Garner suggested, turning around with the cake and blowing out the candles herself. As I looked around, people were diverting their eyes and whispering amongst each other, as they had all night, but now with a new force fueled by our fresh drama.

The whole party followed her, but before heading back in, Dylan shot me a nasty look I don't think I'll ever forget. I just couldn't say anything to him. I couldn't explain it. Why on Earth had I agreed to go out with him? He was never going to be someone to send goosebumps down my spine with the touch of his hand, someone to look at me and cause my heart to ache. He was just Dylan. He was someone else's perfect guy.

Crissy and Melissa didn't head back inside.

"You dumped me for her?!" Crissy demanded again, mounting her hand on her hip and thrusting it to the side. Melissa mirrored her pose, frown and all. They were both shooting laser beams of disappointment like they were super heroes and it was their special power.

"Yes," Brandon said as my heart raced. "I broke up with you because every time I was with you, I wished I was with Kit."

I seriously felt like I had stepped into a cheesy romance novel as my knight in shining armor picked me over the popular girl — but it was incredible at the same time. I had to be dreaming.

"Gross!" Melissa made a revolting face as she turned to leave. "Come on, Crissy, let's get out of here," she said, pulling Crissy's arm to lead her back inside.

"You're going to regret this," Crissy threatened Brandon before disappearing. "She's just a kid," she said looking down at me.

"I don't think so. I think I'll be fine," Brandon whispered as he reached toward me and kissed me fiercely on the mouth. I wrapped my arms around him in a way that I had dreamed of, but never dared act on. When he hugged me back, I knew we'd be more than fine. We were wonderful.

Chapter Twenty-One

I awoke with a panic, certain that last night had been nothing more than a dream. Were Brandon and I truly a couple now? It had all happened so fast. I checked my phone for a text — nothing from Brandon. Then I checked my email, hoping to find some gorgeous love letter, but alas, it was just another day. I turned on my music and lay in bed listening to a mash-up DJ that Brandon liked. It was time to start branching out beyond classic rock.

As I searched for patterns in the popcorn ceiling, my mind drifted down from the clouds and settled back into reality. The house was really quiet. Dad was moving out. I had to tell Mom and Dad about Brandon and me. Mom would wonder about Dylan. I also had to finish studying for finals. I'd sporadically been reviewing my old textbooks for the last two weeks, but it was time to get serious. Whether I was ready or not, they were happening tomorrow. It was amazing that my brain actually stopped stressing about them for a few hours last night. I guess it was on overload. The summer was ending. Life was moving on.

I must have drifted back to sleep because the music had ended and the sun was streaming in with full force through my bedroom windows. My clock radio read 11:00. I rubbed my eyes, tossed back the sheets, and climbed out of bed, feeling groggy from oversleeping.

"Hi, Mom," I said as I walked into the kitchen. She was at her usual station, standing in front of the oven wearing an apron and holding an oven mitt. "Umm, smells good. What are you making?"

"Zucchini bread. Our new neighbors brought a basket full from their garden yesterday."

"Yum." I smiled then opened the fridge looking for orange juice. "It's awful quiet. Has Dad left already?"

Mom nodded, but didn't make eye contact.

"Really?"

"Actually, he left last night." Her tone was apologetic.

I thought he'd at least say goodbye or something," I said, slamming the fridge door shut.

"He wanted to see you," Mom said, trying to reassure me, though I couldn't figure out why she'd want to defend him.

"So where is he going anyway?"

"He's staying with Tim for a while, until he can find an apartment."

"But if you're just separating, why is he getting an apartment?" A new sense of alarm rose within me.

"Oh, Kit!" Mom placed her hands over her face and cried.

I put my arms around her and pulled her to me. "It's not fair that Tyler's death did this," I said, taking the mitt out of her hand.

"Honey, it didn't. I need you to understand this. Everything started way before this summer. We haven't been close for more than a year."

"What?" I said, leaning against a counter for support.

"Tyler's de ... well, Tyler just pushed the issue to the surface — or maybe propelled it, I should say. We were young when we met, Kit," she continued as she regained composure. "We're not the same people. You don't always grow together."

How clueless had Tyler and I been? "So this is really going to mean divorce?"

"Maybe. I don't want to lie to you. We all just need to find happiness again. I'm so thrilled that you found a boy who likes you and who you like back. It brings me so much joy."

I gulped. "Yeah about that, Mom ..."

"Oh, no, did something happen at the party?"

"Yes, something did. But it's all good."

Mom eyed me warily, and suddenly my courage disappeared. "It's about Brandon," I said.

"Oh?" Mom's tone grew in heaviness, and I took a deep breath before continuing.

"Yeah, so ... I'm with Brandon now."

"Brandon!" Mom's surprise caught me off guard. Surely she saw the signs all summer. We'd been completely inseparable since the funeral.

"Uh huh."

"But he has a girlfriend."

"Had a girlfriend," I corrected. Thinking of Crissy in the past tense gave me such a thrill.

"Isn't that a bit ..."

"Bit what?" I demanded, letting go of Mom.

"He's like a brother to you, Kit. He was Tyler's best, oh, this is all too much."

"I've been in love with him forever."

"No you haven't," Mom answered for me.

"Excuse me?" I barked.

"You just miss Tyler. That's what this is about." I didn't say anything. "How long has this been going on?" Mom demanded.

"What does it matter?!" I yelled and started to leave the kitchen. "I'm in love. Can't you be happy for me? I thought I could count on your support at least. Brandon's mom seems to be happy for us."

"I'm not Brandon's mom."

"No, that's for sure," I said as I started walking away.

"What's that supposed to mean?" Mom called after me.

"Nothing. I'm going to the beach." I went upstairs, put on my swimsuit, and then grabbed my phone and called Brandon.

✱ ✱ ✱ ✱

"So," I smiled, taking Brandon's hand in mine. We walked down the boardwalk stairs onto the hot sand. "My mom wasn't so hip to the idea of us together."

"Really? I'm sure she'll come around. She totally loves me."

"Yeah, I think that's the problem. She looks at you like you're her son. So then, in her eyes, I'm sort of dating my brother."

"Eww!"

"It isn't like that? Is it?"

"No, Kit. We are not related in any way. What did your dad say?" Brandon asked as we staked out a spot.

The clouds were hanging low and the sun was trying to push through, casting a muted glow across the sand — perfect sunburn weather. I slathered on the sunscreen to avoid frying. Brandon rubbed more on my back and even though he'd done so all summer, this time his pace was less frantic and his palms seemed to linger. I didn't want him to stop.

"Um, well, I didn't exactly have time to chat with you about this last night, but Dad moved out."

"What?" Brandon stopped rubbing and looked at me. "When?"

"This weekend," I said but just admitting it let loose a flood of tears. The tears weren't because I missed Dad. The way he'd been all summer, I was relieved to have him out of the house. It was more like our family broke when Tyler died, and was still breaking. I didn't know how to stop it from falling apart even more.

Brandon took me in his arms as my tears wet his shoulder. "He and Mom told me at dinner last night that he was moving out today," I continued.

"Unbelievable!"

I nodded. "He didn't even say goodbye. He was gone when I got up today."

Brandon rocked me tight against him. After a while, I came back to the present.

"This is real?" I asked Brandon, drilling into his eyes. "You and me?"

"Yeah, it's real."

I looked at Brandon and thought back to the Fourth of July, the night of the storm, all of our stolen kisses that happened late at night, and how I'd always wished that they could continue in the light of day. I wanted to pinch myself to be sure I wasn't dreaming, but I could give myself a welt and still not totally believe that it was real. Brandon kissed me and then pulled away, the mischievous look in his eye present as ever.

"Race ya?" Brandon smiled, and then we were off, racing into the water just like we had all summer.

Chapter Twenty-Two

My heart quickened as I walked into ACHS for the first time since May. More precisely, the first time since the day Tyler died. Hardly anybody was in the building, leaving the hallways strangely empty; I felt stupid for feeling nervous. I was early, so I went upstairs past the freshman lockers. I remembered where everything was and how the lockers felt so intimidating the first day of my freshman year. Now, here I was, a soon-to-be sophomore. Taking baby steps as I approached Tyler's locker, I leaned against it to keep myself from toppling over. I saw visions of him and Melissa holding hands, and him and Brandon laughing. Tyler, so full of life, so completely unaware that life was so temporary. I checked the time on my phone. It was time for the exam.

"I'm here to take my finals from last semester," I told Mrs. Smith, the secretary who'd worked there since my parents were in high school, which was about 120 years ago.

"It's good to see you, Katrina; I'll let Mr. Cametti know you're here. He'll be administering the final exams today."

"Thanks," I mumbled without getting upset that she called me Katrina. How could I get mad at a little old lady?

Mr. Cametti came out about ten minutes later and, thankfully, he made no reference to Tyler. He was as professional and sterile as always, and I respected him more that day than I ever did when he was teaching algebra. The classroom was freezing in anticipation of another brutally hot day. The summer had gone down on record as being the hottest Atlantic City had seen in nearly a hundred years.

The ice-cold metal on the back of the chair pressed into the space between my halter-top and my lower back as I sat down to start the test. The room was nearly empty. There were about ten other kids, some of whom I recognized, but didn't know very well. Apart from illness, death in the family, or major life catastrophe, the only other people taking finals in August were those students who'd been in summer school. Not the group I usually hung out with.

The tests seemed easier than I'd expected, or maybe I just did better in ninth grade than I'd realized. I was done by one o'clock and hopped on my bike to peddle my way to Dad's shop, although I was tempted to detour for the beach. Dad had called last night and asked if he could take me to lunch after my finals. I couldn't believe he actually remembered that I had to take them.

When I got there, he was already in the parking lot hauling some motors into the back of the rusted red work pickup that read Carlin Marina Supply in stenciled white letters on the side.

"Hey there," he called. "Let me just get these loaded. I have to stop at the dock after I drop you off."

"Leave room for my bike."

"Yup."

The door squeaked as it opened. His truck always had the lingering smell of ocean water and dead fish.

"So, how were your finals today?" Dad asked as he climbed into the driver's side.

"Fine."

"Do you think you did well?"

"Yeah. They weren't really that hard."

"That's good. You're a smart girl."

"Thanks." I wondered how many of these stiff conversations I'd have to tolerate each week.

"Really, you are. I've never had to worry about you." He smiled at me. "I thought we'd head over to The Bay House."

"Sounds good," I said. I didn't add that I hadn't been to The Bay House with him since before Tyler died. Our family used to go there almost every Friday night.

"I can't be gone too long. Mom and I have an appointment later this afternoon with Louise."

"Oh, yeah? You still going to her?" he asked as though he'd moved out months, not days ago.

"Not too much. I guess Louise wants to go over some coping skills with me going back to school next week. Whatever."

"You don't sound too excited," Dad smiled as he backed the truck out of the parking lot.

"Like I said, Mom wants me to go."

"So, how was your date this weekend?"

"Um, well, I guess I need to tell you."

"Tell me what?" Dad's question lingered in the air for a long time as he stared at me. When I learn to drive, I'm going to keep my eyes on the road, thank you very much. It was like a scene from a movie, when they have an entire conversation and you wonder how they haven't hit something or someone.

I hesitated. Dad pressed.

"Kit?"

"I have a new boyfriend."

"Not Derek? Or was it Dylan?"

"Dylan. No, it's not Dylan."

"Was he a jerk to you?" Dad looked like he was getting mad.

"No, no, no, Dylan's fine. It wasn't really about him. I'm … well … I'm dating Brandon."

"No shit!" Dad's reaction was so intense I couldn't tell if he was excited or pissed off.

"Is that okay?"

"Yeah, that's terrific, babe! Brandon's a good kid! I was wondering if you two would ever get together."

"Really?"

"Heck yeah! You two are always doing something together and he talks about you all the time."

"Really?" My voice was jumping an octave with each "Really."

"Good for you two."

I thought about telling Dad how Mom's reaction had been less than supportive, but the lightness of the moment overtook me. Dad was so completely different now that we were out of the house that I truly wondered if life might get back to some sort of normality soon. But more than that, I realized how much of our sadness and anger was tied up in our house — the house where Tyler had lived. Did I dare believe that if we left it, we — me, Mom, and Dad — could all live happily ever after again?

The conversation with Dad continued to be light and fun throughout lunch, and I was actually sad to see him leave when he dropped me off. He seemed like the old Dad again, like a weight had been lifted off his shoulders too. We agreed to have dinner later in the week, and I was genuinely looking forward to it.

When I got back to the house, Mom was a panicked mess, worried that we were going to be late for Louise, but I didn't let her get to me. I was too hopeful about the possibilities ahead.

Chapter Twenty-Three

The night before school started, I couldn't sleep. My sophomore year had arrived, but it seemed like only yesterday that I was in junior high. Even though I'd met with Louise last week specifically to work on my coping skills, I kept agonizing over what would happen. I wasn't sure I would ever be ready for all of the people who would be asking about how life was without Tyler — and all the rest of the people who would be too uncomfortable to talk to me period. I wondered how Brandon and I would act around each other in school. How would others react to seeing us together? I headed into Tyler's room. It was 3:00 a.m. and time to dump some of this onto paper and get it out of my brain.

August 27th

Tyler

I'm exhausted but I can't turn my mind off. Tomorrow, I have to go back to school and I don't know that I'm ready to do this without you. It's been the longest summer of my life. Every day since you've been gone I feel myself breaking and changing in so many ways. I never thought you could actually feel yourself grow up, but I do and it hurts sometimes.

I'm sure you know about Brandon and me by now. I really do like him and I need for you to be okay with that. Just a few weeks ago, I was accusing Melissa of replacing you and here I am with Brandon, in a way proving that we're moving on too. In a lot of ways, what I like about Brandon is that he reminds me so much of you. Sometimes I want to apologize to Melissa, even though she has no idea about the stupid fight with Sherry.

Mom and Dad are so much more tolerable now that they're apart, but there's a quietness to the house that's creepy. With or without a divorce, we may need to move — this house holds too many memories of our family. Did you know that you were really the glue who held us all together? Maybe you did.

The words of Mom's friend Patsy keep ringing in my head: "At least life will go back to normal." Life is not normal, but I think what I have learned is that normal isn't real. Normal is what we think should be real. You're not coming back and I've learned to accept that. So now I have Brandon and Lex, and, of course, Grandma Carlin.

I want you to feel okay about me and go on with whatever you have to do up there. I'm not the same Kit as I was at the beginning of the summer.

215

I know that. I've learned who I am without my twin and I'm gonna be okay.

I'm going to be okay.

All my love, Kit

I closed the book and fell asleep on his bed.

About the Author

Tamara Palmer knew she was going to be a writer before she could even write. As a young girl, she created elaborate dramas with her Barbies for days — even weeks — on end. Later, stories made their way onto pages in her typewriter. Tamara obtained a Bachelor of Arts in English/Creative Writing from Eastern Illinois University and has had a handful of short stories and essays published online and in print. She blogs frequently for greyzone, the career advisement business she founded. Missing Tyler is her first novel.

Tamara lives just outside Chicago with her husband, daughter, and assortment of pets. Visit her website at tamarapalmerauthor.com and find her on Facebook and Instagram. You can also reach her directly at tamara@tamarapalmerauthor.com

Acknowledgments

Missing Tyler was born in a writing group in Lafayette, Colorado in the mid-1990's. I want to thank my early test readers: Savannah, her nanny, Anney, Ros, and Kayla, Megan, and her friends Rachel and Chloe, and Lois Bennett, my first agent, who gave me hope that I really could do this. Thank you for believing in me.

I owe a deep and heartfelt thank you to the core of my Boulder writing group: Ann, Laurel, Suzanne, Monica, Susan, and Gye. You all read and critiqued every chapter, sometimes more than once. I love you all dearly and miss you terribly.

I thank Laura Pritchett, writing coach and editor extraordinaire. My second agent, Stephanie Lehman for her masterful editing and for representing me across all the publishing houses in New York. The myriad of friends who read drafts and cheered me on: Melanie, Carol, Allyn, Carrie, and Allison.

As *Missing Tyler* came out of hibernation for a final clean up and launch, I owe an extreme debt of gratitude to my critique partner, David. You helped me re-establish my writing identity and you keep me motivated.

Thank you to my final round of test readers: Emma, Lena, Victoria, and Ainsley. I thank Beth for her editing, Catherine for her gorgeous cover, and Aunt Judi for her final polishing and amazing wealth of knowledge in the publishing realm. You all got me to the finish line.

Beyond the friends and writing community, and much closer to home, I thank my family: Dad, Mom and Tom, and Rebecca.

To those who couldn't wait out my extended publishing timetable, I can hear you cheering me from the other-side, Aunt Deb, Pam, and Sunny.

And the biggest thank you of all to Rob and Elizabeth. You light up my world and inspire me to never stop creating. It truly takes a village (although maybe it didn't need to take 20 years).

Tamara Palmer

January 2017

MISSING TYLER

Tamara Palmer

Available as Kindle or Paperback

on

Amazon.com

www.tamarapalmerauthor.com

www.facebook.com.tamarapalmerauthor

e-mail: tamara@tamarapalmerauthor.com

Made in the USA
Lexington, KY
10 March 2017